THREE FOUR KILL SOME MORE

A CASEY FREMONT MYSTERY

THREE FOUR KILL SOME MORE

JOHN ACHOR

A CASEY FREMONT MYSTERY

Acacia Imprints

ELKHORN, NEBRASKA

Description: fiction, mystery, female, amateur sleuth

This is a work of fiction. Names, characters, places and incidents are either products of author's imagination or are used fictitiously. Any resemblance to actions or persons, living or dead, events or locales is entirely coincidental.

Paperback ISBN: 978-1-949601-03-9

Kindle ISBN: 978-1-949601-04-6

Library of Congress Copyright Number: 2018909099

Cataloging in Publication Data on file with Publisher.

ACACIA IMPRINTS

John Achor

Email: john@johnachor.com

Author's Links:

BLOG: http://www.johnachor.wordpress.com/

FACEBOOK: http://www.facebook.com/jachor1

TWITTER: twitter.com/caseyfremont

WEB SITE: www.johnachor.com

3rd Edition, 2018

10 9 8 7 6 5 4 3 2 1

READER REVIEWS ABOUT
THREE, FOUR – KILL SOME MORE

As with his first novel, John's second effort makes a great read. It is fast paced, with interesting twists & turns in the plot. I look forward to John's third novel (which I understand he is hard at work writing.)

BOB MCC.

My first venture into mystery novels was John Achor's first book, *One, Two – Kill a Few*, and liked it. So I borrowed a friend's copy of this one and loved it. Fun bunch of characters, fast-paced, intriguing twists - entertaining.

ELAINE

My new friend, Casey, is in more trouble. Big trouble. Luckily she has a good posse to help her out. I was hoping she'd survive again so someday I can read *Five, Six – Deadly Mix*. Once again, couldn't put the book down till I finished it.

CARLENE

I LOVE THIS SERIES! Casey and her group of friends, co-workers, romantic interests, etc. are all so wonderfully entertaining! I really liked how the author brought the first book's murder mystery and the characters over into the second book, but still works as a stand alone for anyone who didn't read or listen to the first. I don't usually like on going series but I find myself excited for the next book. Again, Aisling Gray's narration brings each characters individual characteristics to life!

MICHELLE
(AUDIOBOOK REVIEW)

OTHER BOOKS BY JOHN ACHOR

Casey Fremont mysteries
One, Two – Kill A Few
Three, Four – Kill Some More
Five, Six – Deadly Mix

Alex Hilliard thrillers
Assault on the Presidency

DEDICATION

To my wife Pat for her continued understanding and patience.

ACKNOWLEDGMENTS

My profound thanks go to our three children who always give me inspiration and encouragement. Any number of places like coffeehouses, bagel shops where an author can write. Also, to casinos which provide numerous places where an author can relax while his wife beats up their slot machines.

My thanks also go to a Hot Springs, Arkansas critique group: Danielle Burch, Elizabeth Foster, Pug Jones, John Tailby, Bill White and Madelyn Young (I feel I've missed someone and for that I apologize). This group shared their time, knowledge and expertise providing me with more assistance than an author could expect. If there are any errors in this work, they are mine. If I strayed from the straight and narrow, it was due to writer's license or fictionalization and not pure error.

1

YESTERDAY, ROMEO FOLLOWED CASEY FREMONT TO the building where he knew the TrueTemp Agency was located. *That bastard ex-husband of hers must be late again with the alimony check. She needs to get a temporary job to tide her over until the end of the month.*

Earlier today, he followed her to a building, a place he assumed she was interviewing for a job. Now he watched Casey as she strolled through the nearby mall. He wondered if she received his postcard yet…and tried to imagine her excitement at being faced with a new mystery. Was it too soon to take the next step? Romeo decided it was and melted into the crowd.

2

THE GRIP OF THE MILD WINTER WAS OVER; TEMPS were comfortable and allowed me to put the top down on the Mustang on occasion. My mood was rising as I approached my mailbox. It was empty.

I'm damn tired of waiting for the alimony check from my ex to arrive. Jarvis the Rat's monthly tribute is arriving later every month.

Two days ago I visited the TrueTemp Employment Agency looking for another temp job. I can always rely on good ol' Rutledge Trublood to come through for me. He knows if he doesn't, I'll carry out my threat to tell his wife about the way he fondled me that first time at his agency.

It's always fun to see Becca as well. Though she's only the receptionist, she takes even less guff from Rutledge than I do. She and I have several things in common, among them a love of mystery novels. I turned Becca onto collecting signed first editions from some of the best authors in the field.

"Now Casey," Becca said. "Ain't you glad this meddling ol' black gal put you on to Effie? I mean, seems like you and her have really hit it off."

"You're right," I said. "And, I certainly don't consider it meddling. It was a good move for both of us."

Becca punched the intercom button and announced me. "Rutledge, Casey Fremont is here to see you and she has that look in her eye." She waggled her head toward his office and smiled.

Rutledge pulled his typical strings and got me an interview for the following day and told me to report to a Mr.

Thomasen. I don't like Friday interviews—most bosses are looking forward to getting away for the weekend and tend to cut the discussions short.

* * *

By the time Effie Tremayne got home, I was off the internet and excited to tell her what I learned. "Here's my share of this month's rent," she said when she walked into the three-bedroom condo I share with her.

"Never mind that. Let me tell you about the new job I'll be getting."

Effie did a quick change into her grubbies and went to work in the kitchen. She does some cooking and cleaning, and I give her a break on the rent. It's not rent, it's a mortgage. Jarvis the Rat let me have the condo in the divorce hoping I'd default and he could buy it on the cheap. That's how lawyers think, I guess.

I launched into the story about my decision a few days ago. "I got flat tired of waiting for the alimony check to arrive, so I decided to get a permanent-temporary job. Today Rutledge landed me an interview with a smallish law firm that hires private investigators to dig up dirt."

Effie stopped chopping the veggies and looked at me. "Don't stop now."

"Best of both worlds," I said. "I can use the courses I took in Criminal Justice and learn more about how P.I.'s operate. After our caper last fall—the one you called The Case of the Falling Bodies—I've been thinking about getting a P.I. license."

"Wow," Effie said. "You going to let me work for you?"

"I think that'd be a long ways down the road. Oh, there's another upside about the job. The office is close to Park Plaza Mall—and that…means lunch-hour shopping."

"Let me know if they have jobs open I could do. I wouldn't mind a change of scenery."

We were finishing dinner when Aaron got home. Aaron Kincaid is our other roommate. He's a flight attendant, he's black and he's gay. It took me a long while to get used to all that. In truth, it took me months to begin to overcome my prejudices.

"Aaron," Effie said. "Do you want to work for Casey's private investigator's agency?"

That caught him off guard. He stood in the kitchen doorway, a quizzical look on his face and his mouth open. Effie launched into the details of my upcoming job and ideas about the future.

Later, in my room, I dialed Dennis Epstein's number and got his voice mail. I met him last fall when I worked at the Midtown Atrium Towers Building where a body nearly landed on me. He's a detective sergeant with the Little Rock Police Department and a hunk. Our relationship has blown hot and cold for the past several months. I left a message for him and hoped he would take it as encouraging.

* * *

The next morning, Friday, I put on a business suit with a skirt that stopped well above the knees—that ought to hold his attention long enough to land the job. I was on my way to the law firm located near the intersection of University Avenue and West Markham Street.

I was right about Friday interviews. Mr. Thomasen, the senior partner in the law firm wanted to get away early, so he hired me on the spot. I was now an assistant paralegal at a more than decent salary.

Tracy Marston gave me a quick and dirty rundown on the company and handed me a tri-fold brochure about them. "This will answer most of your questions about the people here. And…" She pulled a report-style folder from her desk, "… and this will explain what the bosses expect around here." The cover page was titled: Thomasen, Sinclair & Westland–Employee Guidelines. I made the mistake of referring to the firm as T, S and W. Tracy corrected me and said, "The partners prefer that all of the names are always used." I would have to remember to use the names around here, but outside the office I was sure I would slip into the abbreviated version.

I tucked both items into my purse, finished the employment paperwork and headed for Park Plaza Mall. I think a small celebration is in order Casey, my girl, I told myself. That thought must have been almost audible, because Tracy's face bore a peculiar look as I left.

3

FRIDAY AND SATURDAY WENT FAST. I TOLD MY roommates everything I knew about the law firm where I'd be working. I read the employee guidelines and asked Effie and Aaron for their opinion of the document which contained only male references and pronouns. That coupled with the fact I assumed from my interview, all women want to be addressed by their first name pointed to an old boys' network. We all agreed. The company seemed to lean toward the sexist side. "These folks need some educating," I said.

Dennis and I managed to squeeze in a date early Saturday evening. We ate dinner at a small Italian restaurant. "Wish I had more time," he said. "But I need to get back downtown. The homicides are piling up."

I smiled and winked at him. "Anything my intrepid band of sleuths and I could help you with?"

"Don't rub it in. You did a good job last fall, but I still wonder how much of it was luck."

I put on a face I hoped would convey a hurt-to-the-quick persona and fiddled with the parmesan shaker in the center of the table. None of this elicited a response so I resorted to words. "How many cases are you working?"

"Just stamped one 'closed' this morning. That leaves me with three open cases."

I summoned up what was close to my total police vocabulary and said, "Run the open cases for me."

"Casey, you know I can't get into details with you." He looked up at me and saw my fingers drumming on the table. It was too much for him, so he continued. "I'm looking at two females and one male victim. One of the females was a pros—a prostitute—on the near west side. Looks like she may have tried to rip off a John and he turned the tables on her. I guess the weirdest of these three is the guy. He was making a phone call at an outdoor kiosk. The killer double-tapped him in the head with a .22 caliber and the shooter was at least ten feet away—no stippling. Strange… for what looks like a contract job. The other female Vic appears to be caught up in a domestic violence dispute."

The look on Dennis' face said: I talk too much. "Too bad you have to go back to work," I said.

We finished our spumoni and left the restaurant. Dennis dropped me at the front door to my building. On the way through the lobby, I remembered no one checked the mail today. Twisting the key in the lock, I swung the small door open and scooped out the contents. Since I wasn't expecting anything important, I tucked the mail under my arm and took the lobby elevator to the eighth floor. Inside my condo, I dropped the mail on the entryway table and joined Aaron and Effie in the living room where they were watching the evening news on a local channel.

4

ON SUNDAY MORNING, THE AROMAS DRIFTING FROM the kitchen woke me. Effie must be busy out there and knowing I might miss breakfast, I hurried through my a.m. rituals. Grubby sweat shorts and a tank top would have to do.

I hurried toward the kitchen and grabbed yesterday's mail as I passed near the front door. Effie and Aaron were already seated at the table, which held a large platter stacked high with pecan pancakes. I slid into my chair and found orange juice and coffee already poured for me.

"I knew the smell of coffee would bring you out," Effie said with a big smile on her face.

I grinned back and stabbed two pancakes from the platter. When they were slathered in butter and drowning in pure maple syrup, I sorted the mail into four piles. Pushing a stack toward Aaron, four to Effie and then I flipped through mine—a couple of bills, three that would go into the shredder and a postcard. The message side was plain except for an angel and hand-printed words—the message made no sense. I tossed it into the shred pile.

There was a single pancake left. "Anyone else want it?" Aaron said pointing to the lone occupant of the platter with his fork.

Effie and I shook our heads, so he speared the morsel and dropped it onto his plate in a single swift motion. He said, "All my mail's junk. Either of you have any contributions for the shredder?"

Effie pushed all her envelopes, except one, toward him. I put my junk mail and the postcard onto his scrap heap. Aaron finished his last bite and reached for the shred pile. At the last minute, the postcard got a reprieve. "What do you make of this?" I said and handed it to Aaron. He read both sides, shook his head and passed it to Effie. Her head movement said no as well.

I re-consigned the card to the junk pile, poured another cup of coffee all around, and started on the Sunday morning paper. We adjourned to the living room, coffee and papers in hand. Aaron detoured through the den where the shredding machine resides.

A few minutes later, I looked at Aaron. "Did you run the mail through the shredder?"

"Nope. It's in the reserved waste basket."

I retrieved the postcard and returned to the living room where I sat staring at it—reading and rereading the words. It still made no sense to me, so I handed it to Effie, saying, "Describe what you see on both sides of the card—out loud."

Effie turned the card over and started. "Well, it's addressed to you." She turned it over. "And—"

"No," I said. "Describe everything. The writing, the printing—in detail."

She continued, "Okay, on the address side is a preprinted stamp, and in the lower left is a copyright notice from the Post Office and the word Recycled."

I sat in my favorite chair, leaning back with my eyes closed. I was visualizing her words.

"Your address is printed on this side," she said. "It's all in lowercase, like those letters I remember at the top of the blackboard when I was in grade school. It's got your name and full address. That's all for the front side. At the top of the back side, it says, 'for me to know and you to find out' followed by three periods."

Aaron said, "That could be an ellipsis."

She continued, "Below the first line there's an angel with a bow and arrow. It's an all black silhouette. And under that, in lowercase printing again—oh, the 'for me to know' part was lowercase as well. This part says, 'you need to go a long, long way to find the arrow' and there's two dashes."

"Describe the angel again," Aaron said.

She did and we guessed at the meaning.

"Besides being an angel," Aaron said, "the figure could be Cupid. Aren't there other names for that character?"

Effie took the lead. "Eros from the Greek and Amor is one from the Romans." She must have seen perplexed looks on our faces and added, "I was just reading a book on mythology. By the way, Cupid is also from the Romans."

"Okay, so what does that figure mean, what does it stand for?" Aaron said. "I'll check the internet for definitions." He returned a few minutes later. "Eros is listed as the God of Desire and Sexual Passion. Amor and Cupid are the Roman counterparts and represent the God of Love."

"They all seem to stand for the same thing," Effie said, looking a bit embarrassed. "Love, sex and desire."

I was still shaking my head. "But what does the figure mean in this context?"

Again, none of us had a clue, so we shifted the discussion to the printed words. We decided that the first line, "for me to know and you to find out..." was a challenge of some sort. The other line made no sense at all. "Read that last line again, Effie," I said.

"Okay. 'you need to go a long, long way to find the arrow.'... And I can't make anything of it. Is Cupid, or whatever we call him—or her—going to shoot the arrow? There's a nursery rhyme where somebody shoots an arrow in the air and doesn't know where it's going to land. Anyone remember who that was?"

Aaron rose and headed for the den again. He was back in a couple of minutes with details on the rhyme. "It was a poem by Wordsworth and doesn't identify the archer, except it's in first person 'I'... and the arrow landed in a tree and he didn't find it for a long time."

It was Effie's turn again. "Could that last line be a riddle?"

"What could it mean?" I said.

We muddled over what a "long, long way" could be—how far? Feet, yards, miles or farther? Were we after a person, a place or a thing? When we solved the clue, what would we find?

Effie named our newest pursuit. "We can call it The Case of the Mysterious Postcard."

That's as far as we got. I tucked the card into a slot in the rolltop desk and we all went back to the Sunday newspaper.

5

ON MONDAY MORNING, ROMEO WATCHED CASEY leave her home. For a moment he was upset because she was accompanied by a tall, slim black man. Then he remembered one of her roommates was black. "I am not sure I like that guy staying in her house," he said to no one in particular.

By taking all the shortcuts he could think of, Romeo was in place to watch Casey again. She entered the small building he assumed was her new place of employment. He still wondered who she worked for—five different businesses were housed here.

After she went in, he edged close enough to the front door to see her go into a first-floor office on the left. When Casey was out of sight, he went into the building far enough to see the name on the door. A law firm, he thought. Not the least like her last job.

Romeo stayed near the building until one-thirty waiting for Casey to go to lunch. On several occasions, he massaged his crotch and felt the rise in his trousers. He saw a pizza delivery boy go in and come out. At two o'clock, he decided her office must have sent out for food.

He was disappointed, because he wanted to see how happy she was at getting the postcard. He was sure it must have been delivered over the weekend and could not imagine that her pleasure would not show on her face. There was not enough time this morning as she left for work. He was not close enough to appraise her features—and besides there was the black guy who distracted him.

Romeo needed to make an appointment this afternoon and was upset he would have to leave without seeing Casey again. Maybe next time, he thought, she will signal me how much she appreciates the message on the postcard and what I am doing for her. He even repeated it aloud. "I am doing all this for you, Casey."

6

MY FIRST DAY ON THE NEW JOB, YESTERDAY, WAS A busy one. So much so the boss ordered out for pizza. He even took care of the tab. Today was shaping up to be the same.

I spent most of the morning, nose buried in law books researching a case the firm was handling. At eleven o'clock, Gretchen Love, the firm's real paralegal, startled me when she said, "Casey, here are some folks you should know."

She introduced Arthur Peligrier as the head of Peligrier & Associates, the investigative firm Gretchen said our boss worked with. A younger man standing behind him looked a great deal like the man shaking my hand.

"I know you," the younger man said. "You're that woman who broke the case over at the Midtown Atrium Towers Building last fall. I watched the progress of the story in the papers. I kept track of it all..."

"He seems so smitten with you that he forgot his manners and hasn't introduced himself," Art Peligrier said. "This is my son, Vince."

The younger Peligrier stammered and reached for my hand. As soon as his fingers closed around mine, I wished he would skip the gesture. His grip was soft and damp, and I couldn't wait to extricate my hand from his grasp.

I glanced between the two men, father and son, and saw a vision that made me draw in a sharp breath. A third man I didn't know was standing so still that he almost blended into the background. What caught my attention was his clothing. If I didn't know the man he reminded me of was dead, I could have sworn he was the one who attacked me in my condo last August. This guy was dressed in black from his turtleneck down to his expensive sneakers. The only thing missing was the ski mask that my assailant wore. And this man was around six-feet-two, which was taller than my nemesis.

The older Peligrier must have seen me staring at the man in black. "Casey," he said, "this is my number one investigator, Falcon."

Falcon stepped forward, shook my hand and said, "Pleased to meet you, Ms. Fremont."

It was obvious he was listening to the earlier introductions, yet I didn't see him until we were past that stage. "Please, call me Casey. Is Falcon your first or last name?"

"Both. It's just Falcon," he said.

I couldn't shake my curiosity. "How come Falcon?"

"Did you ever watch a falcon hunt?" When I shook my head, he said, "I'll describe it to you in detail some day."

I wanted to ask more, but his demeanor said: That's all for now.

Art Peligrier sat down with Gretchen Love and me and outlined where they were on a particular case. He laid out the legal research he needed. All the while, young Vince stood behind his father, leering. The son was creeping me out.

After they left, I said to Gretchen, "Does Vince always look and act like a geek?"

"What do you mean?" she said.

"The way he lurks around and seems to hover about six inches off the floor. And the bit of knowing so much about me. Creepy."

At this point I learned that she was far more diplomatic than I am. She said, "He's not so bad once you get to know him." Then she let her head go like a bobble-head doll and rolled her eyes up until nothing but white was showing.

The gesture told me she might be as catty as the rest of us. I mentioned Falcon and how well he looked in that black jersey turtleneck. "Rather formfitting—and a good form for it to fit."

Gretchen did another eye roll. This time her smile said it was one of appreciation. I wondered if Falcon ever dated clients.

"How often do they come by?" I said.

"One or another usually stops in most days."

I hope it's Falcon, I thought.

7

ROMEO WAS ABLE TO FOLLOW OR BE NEAR CASEY FOR most of the week. It was Thursday now, and he was again disappointed.

Casey did not display any hint of appreciation for his actions. He thought she would at least show a smile of recognition, of being happy with the attention he was showering on her.

After all, he thought, I went to a great deal of troubleshooting the man at the pay phone. I expended an inordinate amount of effort and the cunning I used was that of a consummate killer.

He did indeed go out of his way to cover his tracks. He staked out a number of outdoor phone booths and kiosks. The kiosk provided a better opportunity for a kill shot. The frame of the booths might cause a bullet to go astray.

With that decision out of the way, Romeo selected two likely spots. His gun was an old one, but in pristine condition. The Colt Woodsman automatic lent itself to the homemade sound suppressor he designed. During its life, the weapon was passed through so many hands, and unrecorded transactions, before he purchased it, it would be untraceable...And if traced, he had an answer for that as well.

When a hapless victim presented himself at the preferred kiosk, Romeo pumped two bullets into the man's head. He was careful to keep the weapon within the confines of the car so ejected shell casings would land inside. Driving away from the scene, he came close to having an orgasm.

Before the shooting, he cleaned the gun, including the inner working parts, the magazine and the shell casings and bullets. All the while, he wore latex gloves.

When the deed was over, he ran a rat-tail file down the barrel several times and disassembled the weapon. He also struck the receiver with a small hammer so the firing pin and extractor area were disfigured.

A trip along the Arkansas River afforded ample opportunity to dispose of the pieces. He put a minimum of a half-mile between each part of the gun, the file, the hammer and the shell casings. The authorities would have to dredge the river over a stretch of several miles and they still would not find anything. Romeo was pleased and smiled to himself.

He drove back into town and parked the car. Considering his actions, Romeo tried to think of something he missed. He was satisfied no clues were left behind and nothing about the murder could be traced to him.

He drove out Chenal Parkway and delivered the postcard. The one addressed to Casey Fremont. Then, he returned the stolen car back to the neighborhood where he found it.

All those actions were now in the past, he thought, and Casey was not appreciative enough. It was time for Romeo to select another tribute to Casey.

8

BY FRIDAY, I WAS READY TO GIVE UP HOPE THAT A rep from the Peligrier Agency would make an appearance. At midmorning they showed up, and I was disappointed. Instead of Falcon, it was the owner's son, Vince.

I did my best to bury my nose in the law books I was researching but was unable to escape. Acknowledging his greeting, Vince took a seat in the chair nearest my desk.

"Casey, tell me all about those killings you were involved in. I read everything in the papers, but there's no substitute for a firsthand account."

"I'm pretty busy right now. Perhaps some other time." As soon as the words passed my lips, I knew it was a gross error in judgment. The look on his face said: It's a date. When?

Before he could get his mouth in gear, I added, "I really don't like to talk about it." Which was a lie. Most of the time I was ready to regale audiences at the slightest hint of interest. I still couldn't identify an exact reason, but Vince continued to send shivers up my spine.

"Is there someone you need to see," I said. He shook his head and continued to sit there, saying nothing. After a few minutes he became engrossed in cleaning his fingernails. I returned my attention to the book in front of me, but my concentration was shot. By eleven-thirty, I couldn't stand it any longer. I stood, grabbed my purse and announced a bathroom break. I left Vince glued to the same chair, his attention apparently riveted on a right pinky hangnail.

I stopped at Gretchen's desk. "I'm taking an early lunch. You can reach me at the Mall—I'll have my cell on in case the fit hits the Shan." I could tell by her expression that this old punch line was lost on her. "Call me if there's an emergency," I said.

* * *

In the Park Plaza Mall, I covered the women's department at two of the larger stores and was contemplating lunch. The debate between a pretzel from Aunt Annie's and Chinese in the food court was heating up. Orange chicken and rice won out, so I headed down the stairs to the lower level.

A voice behind me said, "You're safe, Casey. I do not see any falling bodies."

I turned. "Gene Morse. What are you doing here?" My mind raced back to the day I interviewed at Cyber-Technology in the Midtown Atrium Tower building. Gene was my Good Samaritan, the person who shoved me out of the path of a man plunging to his death in the atrium.

He said, "Did I ever apologize for sending you sprawling that day?"

"No need. If old Hawkins had landed on me, I might not be here to apologize to. I'm grateful to you."

We reminisced for a few minutes. Then he told me he was between client appointments, stopped here to pick up a dress shirt and grab a bite to eat. The plastic bag with a men's store logo on it confirmed his purchase. He opted for Italian, I got Chinese, and we shared a table for lunch. The smells of ravioli and orange chicken mingled into a pleasant combination.

Gene asked me about my jobs since I left that position at Cyber-Tech. I found myself doing the babbling brook number. I told him about Effie getting started in dress design and the architecture courses Aaron was taking. I couldn't brag enough about them.

"That is all well and good," he said. "But what have you been up to?"

Again, the words rippled over the rocks, as I shifted to talking about myself. I shared with him my reasons for looking for a more permanent job—maybe a career. Between asking him a couple of questions, I described the people in the firm and the detective agency. I didn't bother to talk about the office or the type of work I was doing. I made sure I omitted details about creepy old Vince. A glance at my watch surprised me—the time was flying by. "Now tell me about you," I said.

"I really need to get going." He rose and said, "I will see you later." Turning, he melted into the throng of shoppers.

That's just like him. This happened before. I tell him all about me and learn nothing about him. Do I babble too much or is he just good at drawing people out? I decided that would have to remain a rhetorical question.

* * *

Tracy handed me a phone message when I returned to work. She also confirmed Vince was gone. That was a pleasant surprise. Seated at my desk, I read the words on the pink slip. It was from Falcon and the message, which Tracy enclosed in quotes, "See you at Augustinos' at 5:30." More of an order than an invitation—and no return phone number. I was ready to toss it but decided to show up and give him a piece of my mind for being so rude.

I left a message on my home machine to let my roomies know I wouldn't be there for supper. I figured whether he bought me dinner or I paid for it myself, I'd be late. Before hanging up, I checked for messages on my answering machine. The usual telemarketer calls and one from Jarvis, my ex.

He sounded almost desperate but that was one of Jarvis' common ploys—figuring the pathetic approach would garner attention. The "please, call me as soon as you get this…please," almost hooked me. Two "pleases" in one sentence was unusual. Then my married life did a fast-forward through my brain. When

I got to the part where he dumped me and took up with Bambi, I decided—to hell with him, he can wait his turn. Right after I chew Falcon out, I'll give Jarvis a call.

* * *

I was familiar with Augustinos'. This small restaurant and bar was a short distance from my workplace and it took only a few minutes to drive there. Like most neighborhood establishments, the parking was limited and I drove around the block twice before I located a parking spot. The time read five thirty-five when I pushed the front door open and entered. I saw Falcon sitting at a table for two in a back corner of the bar area.

He stood as I approached his table. "I'm glad you could make it—nearly on time."

His demeanor left me cold. The greeting was as rude as his initial invitation. "Consider yourself lucky I bothered to show at all."

He tilted his head back and laughed from way down deep. I was startled at his reaction but pleased to see the man had a sense of humor. I looked him over as he slid a chair out for me. Still wearing all black, I couldn't tell if it was a different outfit or the same one he wore to our office during that previous visit. I guessed he had any number of the same turtlenecks, slacks and shoes. If nothing else, the man was intriguing and my hostility was melting like a lump of sugar in hot coffee.

The waitress took our order. I was having white wine and he ordered Chivas Regal scotch neat. When the drinks arrived, he began asking questions. It felt like an interrogation and I told him so.

"Sorry," he said. "Old habits die hard…and it's been a long time since I asked a woman out."

"Oh, then this is a date?"

I might have picked up on the wrong signal, but I thought for a moment his face flushed. Whatever it was, it disappeared fast. "Cat got your tongue?" I said.

"No. Just appraising the situation."

"You don't talk much, do you?"

He folded his cocktail napkin into quarters and stared at me. "Occupational hazard."

"This is the weirdest version of small talk I've ever heard."

"Sorry again. What would you like to say…or ask me?"

I took the offer. "Tell me about your name. How come they call you Falcon?"

"Okay. My real name is Roberto Falcone. I never liked it much, so I took the ethnic vowel off the end and dropped the first name. One more thing…" He made sure I was looking at him and finished the sentence. "I don't share that with many, so I'd like to think you won't spread the details around."

I nodded an assent. "The other day you said you'd tell me about how falcons hunt."

"That I did." He unfolded his cocktail napkin and smoothed it out on the table. "Falcons circle at great heights on silent wings. They have keen eyesight and when they spot some prey, they fold their wings and dive leaving only enough wing extended to have stability and guidance. Before the target hears the wind rushing over feathers, the bird extends his legs and the talons encircle the prey and he is again the successful hunter."

"Is that you? Is that what you do for a living?"

He was quiet for several minutes. At last he said, "Yes, I suppose that's a good description of what I do."

We talked for hours. I blurted out subjects and details that surprised me because I felt comfortable with this man. Falcon didn't share as much as I did, but I think he went beyond his usual boundaries. I mentioned the peculiar postcard I received.

He asked me to describe it and was quiet for a long time before he spoke. "I could check it for fingerprints…if you'd like me to."

I told him that was a good idea and he said he'd stop by over the weekend to pick it up. The clock over the bar caught my attention for the first time and I was amazed to see it was ten-thirty. "I really have to get home," I said.

He asked if I would like company on the way home. When I shook my head, he swept up his change, stood, dropped several bills on the table, and strolled toward the entrance. Well, I thought. Nothing like ignoring the usual amenities. Guess I can't blame him—I said I didn't need company.

It was after eleven when I walked into my home. I saw the answering machine light blinking and thought of Jarvis. "I don't have the stamina for you tonight," I said to the machine.

"What was that?"

It was Effie's voice coming from the den. I poked my head in there and saw she was working on a sketch of a dress. "I was talking to Jarvis," I said. "He'll just have to wait until tomorrow."

9

LAST WEDNESDAY, I GOT HOME SO LATE I DIDN'T bother to return the phone call from Jarvis. I must be getting mellower. In the past, whenever I referred to him, in thoughts or aloud, it was always Jarvis the Rat. He left messages on Thursday and Friday, which I ignored as well. The word desperate was prominent in each message. Jarvis tends to be over-dramatic, even more so when referring to himself. Since I had no plans for the day, except my semi-official Saturday night date with Dennis, I planned to give Jarvis a call this afternoon.

PK made his grand entrance into the living room and interrupted my solitude. He startled me enough I dropped my newspaper. PK is short for Psycho Kitty, which best describes his behavior. Part of it's not his fault. There is a large mural in the living room featuring a table in front of a window. After numerous ill-fated attempts, he has not learned. It's—streak—splat—slide. His leap is well-timed and the height is correct. I can't imagine what goes through a cat's mind when he hits the wall and slides to the floor. He shook his head and stared at me with that I-meant-to-do-that look. I went back to my reading and PK wedged himself next to me in our favorite recliner.

My reading was interrupted again when the doorbell rang. Damn, I thought. I bet Jarvis got tired of leaving messages and decided to come by in person. I was relieved when I opened the door and saw Falcon standing there. As usual, he was wearing all black. Today he added a sport coat to his attire.

"I came for that postcard," he said.

I led him inside and pulled the card from the slot in the rolltop desk. He took it by the edges, between his thumb and forefinger. With his other hand, he fished a plastic bag from his jacket pocket.

Falcon said, "Open this for me."

He took the bag back and sealed the card inside. "I'll process it for fingerprints and get back to you in a few days. Who else lives here?"

"Another lady and a gentleman. Effie Tremayne and Aaron Kincaid." I expected at least a raised eyebrow when I mentioned a gentleman. His face might have been concrete for all the information it conveyed.

"Are they here?"

When I nodded, he said, "I'd like to get their fingerprints."

I called their names and they joined us in the dining room. When the introductions were complete, Falcon produced two cards and a small leather case from an inside pocket. It took him about one minute to roll out some black paste on a sheet of glass, press Effie's fingers into the ink and onto one of the cards.

Aaron jerked his hand back when Falcon reached for it. "What the hell is this for?" he said.

Falcon explained he wanted to be able to eliminate the three of us from any prints he discovered on the postcard. "Actually, young man, I could get your prints on-line—you were in the Air Force weren't you?" He didn't wait for an answer. "This is faster." Falcon took Aaron's hand and recorded his prints on a second card.

The look on Aaron's face mirrored my thoughts. How did Falcon know about Aaron in the first place?

Falcon, the apparent mind reader said, "I always research the folks I work with." He turned to Effie and said, "How's the clothing design business coming along?"

Effie stared at him. Falcon passed a hand wipe to Aaron. "Are your architectural courses teaching you what you want?"

"I'm almost afraid to ask what you know about me," I said.

"You're right. You don't want to know."

I could swear he almost winked. But the fifth face on Mt. Rushmore was hard to interpret. "Aren't you going to take my prints?"

He looked at me. "I got them from the wineglasses you used Wednesday night. The bartender is a friend of mine." Falcon gathered his tools and cards and stored them in his pockets. "Perhaps, some evening over a glass of Chablis, I could fill you in…I'll see myself out."

I was still mulling over his offer—it was an offer, wasn't it?—as I watched his back depart through the front door.

* * *

I was thinking about the return call I owed Jarvis but was putting it off. After supporting him through law school while I shelved my own ambitions, he told me to stay home like a good little wife. I spent eight years sitting at home only to learn that he was having an affair with his secretary. When he hired her, I should have been suspicious—how many women do you know named Bambi? He dumped me for her, got a divorce and has been ducking the monthly alimony payments. I wasn't anxious to discuss anything with him.

For the second time today, the doorbell jarred me out of my reverie. This time it *was* Jarvis. He insisted we go to a small coffee shop nearby. Sitting across the booth from him, I still harbored reservations, but did my best to figure out what was bothering him. He was talking like his life depended on it—and he was rambling, making no sense. I got tired of playing with the knives, forks, saltshakers and napkins and held up my hand—palm toward him. His eyes moved from his lap to the window and back again. I began to wonder if he would ever become coherent and still placing my hand out closer to his face, I shouted, "Whoa."

He paused in midsentence and looked at me. "Wh… wh…what?"

"Slow down and get to the point. I don't plan to sit here all afternoon waiting for you 'cause I've got a date tonight."

"Bambi left me. I caught her screwing around. She's filing for divorce." That statement brought a flood of tears and sobbing from him. I couldn't keep a straight face. I didn't want him to see my smile and was glad he was staring at his lap again.

"What did you expect from someone who screwed you while you were married to me?"

"That was different."

"Oh, really. And just how was it different?" His mouth opened, but no words came out. In my mind, there was an image of chickens roosting, and droppings all over his apartment—I stifled another guffaw. "I'll tell you what's different. Last time it was you banging your secretary on your desk when I walked into your office. You got caught—you were the dumper and I was the dumpee. Now you are the dumpee. Don't feel very good does it?"

"I'm sorry for everything." The sobs were still coming. "Casey, you have to take me back. We can get married all over again."

"I don't think so. Don't forget to keep those cards and letters—and more important—those checks coming in the mail."

"Casey, I'm desperate. If you don't take me back, I'm not responsible for what I might do."

I stood up. "Grow up Jarvis. It ain't gonna happen." I turned around and left the coffee shop.

10

WEDNESDAY MORNING, THE INTERCOM ON MY phone rang and it was our receptionist, Tracy Marston. "Someone from the Peligrier Agency to see you, Casey."

She broke the connection before I could ask who it was. I jumped up thinking, Falcon. My pace slowed as an image of Vince Peligrier flashed in front of me. I turned the corner to the reception area and couldn't move fast enough. Even from the back, I knew the man in black must be Falcon. I was four feet from him when he whirled to face me. The carpet in the office is so thick he could not have heard me approaching.

"Is there somewhere we can speak in private?" he said.

Glancing over my shoulder, I saw our small conference room was empty. I led him there, though my impression of him is: no one leads Falcon anywhere he doesn't want to go.

Seated side-by-side at the table, Falcon pulled an evidence envelope from a jacket pocket. Pointing to the postcard visible through the plastic, he said, "There are three sets of fingerprints on that."

Now we're getting somewhere, I thought.

Falcon must have read my expression, because he apologized for raining on my smiley face. "Sorry," he said. "The prints belong to you and your two roommates."

"Bummer."

Falcon smiled and told me, although we don't know who delivered the card, we know something about him or her. "Let's refer to the mystery person as a 'him.' I hate all that PC crap." He told me there should have been at least one more set of finger-prints on the card—the postman. "Since they don't appear and there's no postmark, we know the author delivered it himself. He knows where you live and your condo ID—I checked your building. Names don't appear on the mailboxes in the lobby."

I sat there internalizing the information—wondering who would send me a card like this. Was it someone playing a joke on me? Or, did this somebody have more serious intentions?

Falcon said, "Do you have any idea who could have sent it?" When I shook my head, he continued. "At this point, I don't think you have anything to be concerned about. If you get a second one, I want you to contact me at once—no matter what time of day it is." He handed me a card with the outline of a bird of prey and two numbers on it. One was listed as "cell" and the other as "pager."

We arranged to meet after my work hours. He asked me to pick the spot this time.

* * *

The evening was similar to our first date. Falcon and I lost track of time, and enjoyed our drinks and dinner. It was late when I got back to my condo. A blinking light on my answering machine signaled messages that turned out to be from Dennis and Jarvis. Dennis called looking for confirmation of our dinner date for Saturday night. Jarvis was his usual whiny self, pleading for me to remarry him.

I considered the two. Dennis fit the tall, dark and handsome category. Jarvis was good looking enough, but I spent eight years with him before he deserted our marriage.

I practiced married names in my head. Mrs. Dennis Epstein—I smiled. Mrs. Jarvis Parnell Sheffield the Third—the look on my face might have accompanied a sour stomach.

Perhaps it's time to expand my horizons. I remembered the trysts with Dennis and left a voice mail for him okaying Saturday night. I ignored the one from Jarvis.

Then I thought, Mrs. Falcon...I cocked my head and smiled.

11

HOPING TO SLEEP IN, I DID NOT HIT THE ALARM button last night. I woke early without the buzzer going off.

The drapes were closed, so I stumbled to the window to get my first glimpse of the day. I squinted my eyes to shield them from the sun's glare as it crawled above the horizon.

Nothing. I unscrunched my eyes—still nothing. With my eyes wide open, I greeted a dismal day—storm clouds rolling in from the west and the wind driving the rain at a diagonal. I opened my window and the fresh smell of rain eased the burden of the morning. "I got a feeling this is going to be a lousy one." PK stared at me but didn't say anything.

Most of the time, Aaron's job as a flight attendant only took him out of town for two or three days at a time. Today, he was on the last of a five-day trip. That left Effie and me to fend for ourselves. I'm terrible as a chef, Effie's a lot better, but Aaron, when he puts his mind to it, puts both of us to shame.

I managed a pot of coffee and was sitting at the kitchen bar with a cup and the morning paper. Footsteps came padding from the living room toward me. Not unusual. All of us tended to go barefoot at times. I assumed it was Effie since Aaron was out of town.

The footsteps stopped at the entrance to the kitchen. I looked up and saw a large black man wearing only a pair of white boxer shorts—and it wasn't Aaron. I jerked the cleaver from its nesting spot in the countertop holder and brandished it about shoulder height. The man's eyes grew large and his hands went up, palms toward me.

He gasped, "Whoa, lady…"

I shouted in the most ferocious voice I could muster, "Who the hell are you?"

Before he could answer, the name Tim was shouted twice. It was Aaron's voice. Now I was confused in a major way. Aaron stepped in front of the man I assumed was Tim and said, "You can put the meat cleaver down, Casey."

I did as suggested, and he continued. "I should have cleared our sleepover with you, I guess."

"You don't have to do that. We're all adults...but I would appreciate a little warning."

Aaron pointed to the small dry-erase board on the front of the fridge. I read it for the first time this morning: Casey, I got back a day early and I have a friend staying over with me, Aaron.

Tim said, looking at Aaron, "I smelled the coffee and you weren't in the bedroom. I figured you were out here."

"I was in the bathroom," Aaron said, "and when did you start running around other people's homes in your skivvies?"

Tim looked down at himself and did a one-hand fig leaf cover-up. "I'm sorry Ms. Fremont. I usually have more manners than this."

"We've already been intimate enough that you can call me Casey." He looked even more embarrassed but we all laughed.

Aaron looked down and realized he was dressed in a similar manner...I compared the two in my mind. They were both the same height and build. The washboard abs on the two of them said they worked out on a regular basis. Aaron lighter, almost a dusty skin tone set them apart. Tim's complexion was deep ebony. I realized there was much I didn't know about blacks.

I said, "If the two of you will put on some clothes, I'll share the coffee."

We were laughing as they turned to go back to Aaron's room. They passed Effie when she entered the kitchen rubbing her eyes. I spent the next few minutes bringing Effie up to speed about Aaron and Tim.

Later, we were getting ready for lunch. Effie and Aaron were doing the honors in the kitchen and I completed the drinks—tumblers of water—and put them on the table when the phone rang. It was my ex, Jarvis.

"Casey," he said, "you've got to listen to me. I'm desperate."

He droned on like an old-time congressman filibustering the Senate. Somehow, he learned to inhale while continuing to talk at the same time. I listened until I was bored and then banged the receiver on the table. When I put the earpiece back to my head, he was silent. "You've been carrying on, but you still haven't told me why you are so desperate. There couldn't be trouble in paradise, could there?"

"Casey, Bambi left me. She's moved out. I tried to get her to come back, but she said it was over."

"Life's a bitch, Jarvis. And you've already told me all of this." He whined for a while and I reminded him of my warnings when he dumped me. I wanted to say, Nayh, nayh, nayh, nayh, nayh-nayh—told you so. I resisted and gave myself a mental pat on the back.

He broke into my mental machinations and told me again he was desperate. He wanted me to take him back. He said he would do anything—anything to get back together. "If I can't have you, Casey, I'll—"

That's where I told him to grow up, that I needed to get ready for a date and slammed the phone down.

Ten minutes later the phone rang once more. Thinking it was Jarvis again, I let the machine pick up. When I heard Dennis' voice, I broke in apologizing for screening calls.

He said, "Sorry, gal, but I've got to break our date tonight. There's been a gory one I have to investigate. I won't have any spare time for days."

We commiserated for a few minutes. I heard someone in the background shout his name. "Sorry, gotta go," was all he had time to say.

Yep, the day started dismal and was getting worse by the hour. I perked up a bit when Effie put toasted BLTs on the table for all of us. After lunch, Tim excused himself, telling us he needed to get back to his house and left.

Aaron retired to his room and Effie and I finished the paper. She announced she was going to check the mail.

Minutes later, the front door banged open and Effie raced in heading for the kitchen. She returned with a large Ziploc bag and bamboo tongs in her hand. Grabbing me by the arm, she dragged me toward the front door.

"Whoa," I said. "What the hell's going on?"

"There's another postcard in the mailbox. C'mon, let's go get it."

In the lobby, she used the tongs to remove the card and drop it into the baggie. "Falcon told me to call him if I got another one of these," I said. I did, but the elevator killed the signal on my cell phone. In my condo, a second call to Falcon was successful.

Thirty minutes after I completed my conversation with Falcon, he was walking through our front door. He used our tongs and transferred the card to an evidence bag.

I hated to turn the postcard loose and watch it walk out the front door. "Will a scanner affect any prints on it?"

He shook his head and said, "Use the tongs to get it in and out of the bag. Be sure to handle it by the edges and don't slide it around on the scanner glass—that could degrade latents. Other than that…" He smiled and held the evidence container at arm's length toward me.

I kept the scanned copy of the second card and handed Falcon the original. On his way out, he handed me another clear bag. This one held the first postcard I received.

12

MY TWO ROOMIES AND I SCRUTINIZED THE TWO
sheets from my all-in-one printer-scanner that contained a single
side of the latest postcard. I compared the front of this new one
with the first. They were identical down to my address printed
in lower case letters. The back sides were different.

The printing at the top of this newest postcard read:

```
i am doing this all for you casey

ask dennis why he is so busy
```

Centered in the middle of the card was the silhouette of a
black cat, facing to the right with its back arched and the tail up
in the air. Below that my secret admirer wrote, again in lowercase:

```
lizzy borden and the brick layer — —
```

"What's a bricklayer got to do with Lizzy Borden?" Aaron said.

No one responded. "The front side of both cards look alike—a
lot alike." Effie said. "I mean almost exactly alike."

I took the first card, scanned the front and returned to
the dining room table. I marked this copy with the number
one, handed it to Effie and said, "Lay one on top of the other
and hold them up to the light." Aaron flicked on the light fix-
ture over the table and Effie held the papers between her eyes
and the lamp. "Now line up the paper so the preprinted parts
match," I said.

When the papers were in position, she said, "Your printed address is almost exactly the same."

Aaron peered over her shoulder. "She's right. They're close, but I don't think they were printed on a computer."

I said, "I wonder if Falcon checked the ink on the first card."

"How or why does someone print two cards that look like duplicates?" Aaron said.

Effie jumped in. "He's obsessive-compulsive or anal-retentive or something like that. I think it tells us he's a precise planner and meticulous. That's why he doesn't leave fingerprints on the cards. This one doesn't have a postmark, and I bet Falcon doesn't find any prints on this second card either."

I screwed my face into what was supposed to be a puzzled look. "How do you get postcards with no fingerprints on them?"

Aaron spoke out. "You buy a stack of them at a Post Office. The clerk only touches the top and bottom ones and you can toss those two away. The rest are fingerprint free. Wear gloves when you handle them and voilá—no prints."

Effie looked worried. "I think this guy is a stalker."

"You might be stretching for such a conclusion," I said.

"Don't take it too lightly," she said. "I've done some reading on the subject of stalkers and he fits the bill. Look, he's trying to get your attention with the cards. Whatever he's doing,—according to him—it's all for you, Casey. He's been to the lobby of our building twice. He's hanging around looking for attention from you. I don't think that's a stretch."

I was thinking along the same lines and did my best to ignore it. Several of the Criminal Justice courses I took while I was the no-wife-of-mine-will-work married lady, touched on the stalker problem. I felt a shiver run up and down my spine.

* * *

Falcon called and before he could report, I said, "No prints on this card either — right?"

If he was surprised, it didn't show in his voice. "How did you come to that conclusion?" he said.

I went over the suppositions my intrepid team of investigators came up with. He told me we were on the right track all the way down the line.

I said, "No prints—he delivered the second card himself. That means he's been in the lobby of my building twice and I'm creeped out."

"Casey, I don't think you have anything to worry about for now. He seems to be doing his best to impress you rather than harm you." He waited for me to answer, but I couldn't think of anything to say. "Spend some time attempting to figure out the messages on the cards. To be on the safe side though, don't be alarmed if you see an Hispanic with a ponytail and a red bandanna in your rear view mirror or standing nearby."

"What 'dya mean don't be alarmed? Who will that be?"

"He's a freelancer I hire on occasion. Don't let his lack of stature fool you. He can be one mean dude when he needs to be."

"That sure is reassuring." I hoped my sarcasm came through to him. "In case I need to say hello, what's his name?"

"Ralphie. Oh, I'm about the only one who can get away with using his nickname. You better call him Raphael. It's Raphael de Jesus."

I hung up. I long ago gave up waiting for the usual ending one expects on the phone or in person. Falcon didn't adhere to many of the conventions of polite society. When he's done, he's gone.

I reviewed my conversation with Aaron and Effie. "I feel better knowing someone other than the card sender is looking over my shoulder…I guess."

* * *

Sunday morning came and went. The paper was in several heaps around the living room. Effie left the room and returned with the evidence bag containing the first postcard and the scanned pictures of the second one.

"We still haven't figured out what these two messages mean," she said.

"I'm not sure we can go any further. We don't have any idea what he is referring to," I said.

Aaron moved across the room and sat next to Effie. "He must be someone you know, Casey. Think back—who do you know who could be doing something to impress you?"

I shook my head. "I don't have the foggiest. I haven't even met anyone new in quite a while."

Aaron pressed his point. "Okay. So no who, how about a why. Maybe it's not someone new. How about good old Jarvis? He's been after you recently."

"That's true..." I shook my head back and forth in slow motion. "but I don't give him credit to come up with anything like this. Even though he's a lawyer, I don't think he's bright enough to turn the boot upside down looking for the instructions."

Effie took the lead. "Well, since this approach doesn't seem to be working, let's try to figure out what the messages mean." She left the room again and returned with enough copies of both cards for all of us.

We studied without speaking. The silence spoke for us. No one had a clue. Starting with the first card, we brainstormed the wording—Cupid, Eros, Amor, arrow, dart—until we were repeating the same words.

"Lizzy Borden," Aaron said, "suggests an ax. Remember the rhyme? 'Lizzy Borden took an ax and gave her father forty whacks. When she saw what she had done, she gave her mother forty-one.' Do we know anyone who has been axed recently?"

More head shakes. "Well, then back to the first one." He repeated the list of words we covered earlier, then said, "What if it's none of those. What if it's about the person's action—someone who shoots arrows—an archer? Do we know anyone who is good with a bow and arrow? Or...do we know anyone named Archer or Bowman?"

Effie and I both said no and Aaron shook his head as well. He repeated the words from the first card, " 'Go a long, long way to find the arrow.' Define a long, long way."

"Miles and miles," Effie said.

"Miles to find an arrow?" I said.

"Forget the arrow for a minute. Look at the type of character—an archer—and the distance—miles. Does that suggest a name?"

Aaron was leaving me in the dust, but Effie gave it a shot. "Archer Miles...oh...Miles Archer. Is that who you mean?"

"Who's Miles Archer?" I said. The two of them grinned and encouraged me to think back. "Oh...Sam Spade's partner in *The Maltese Falcon*. That's a long stretch, isn't it?"

"Maybe not," Aaron said. "Didn't you tell us that one of the cases Dennis was investigating involved a man shot while making a call in a phone booth?"

I started to speak, but Aaron beat me to it. "That's the way Miles Archer died—shot in a phone booth. I realize it's a long way round robin's barn, but a murder described on the postcard is tied to you, Casey—Dennis is investigating it."

Effie said, "What other murders is he looking into?"

I looked up. "Something about a prostitute, or her John and...I don't remember the others."

Aaron said, "The latest card told you to ask Dennis why he's so busy. That might suggest a new murder. Did he mention one?"

"He said he would be busy and it was a gory case."

"Like maybe someone used an ax?" Effie said. "And, I should have solved that first clue. I'm the namesake of Sam Spade's secretary, Effie Perrine. I've always thought my mother got the idea for my name from the Sam Spade story."

* * *

Later in the afternoon, it took four phone calls and voice mail messages before I reached Dennis. I asked him to tell me about his latest case—in police-ese, I told him to run the case.

"Damnit, Casey, you know I can't get into details with civilians."

"Okay. Then just answer one question. Does this one involve an ax?"

"Holy crap, we haven't released any details. How did you know that?"

"Me and my crack investigative team figured it out." I knew it would be tough to wheedle the details from Dennis.

13

I LIKE TO THINK IT'S MY GIRLISH CHARMS WHICH made Dennis give up and talk to me. In reality, my gut says he was sorry he cancelled our date last night. Whatever the reason, he agreed to go over the cases he was working.

"You know I can't get into any evidentiary details, but beyond that what do you want to know?" he said.

"Can you tell me the dates of your cases and how they died in general?" I held my breath and wondered if I asked for too much.

"Since the last one I closed, I now have four opens. The first of those was a hooker. I think I told you we suspect her date for the evening did it—best guess is that she tried to roll him and he didn't roll very well. She was strangled."

"Where?"

"A cheap, warm-sheet motel on the near west side."

"When?"

"Let's see, I caught that one on the…the sixth…ah, that would have been a Wednesday.

"The next one," he said, "was the lady who was the victim of domestic abuse—she got it the following Tuesday, the twelfth. We're pretty sure her live-in boyfriend did it, but he's in the wind. We have some leads, but it will take luck to nail him."

When I didn't say anything, he went on, "The one after that was the guy who looked like a contract shooting—shot with a .22 caliber. He caught two in the head while he was making a call from an outside phone. Very clean, no shell casings, no forensic evidence…"

His pause told me he was concerned about how much he was telling me. "When did he die?"

"He was killed two nights later, Thursday, the fourteenth and from the papers you no doubt know where he was shot."

I did recall the news reports detailing the location. I didn't remember the exact street, but doubted the location affected my admirer's deeds. "How about this last one, the gory one I think you called it."

"Yeah," Dennis said. "That one came in yesterday—a woman hacked to death with an ax or hatchet. Hacked may be an over-statement. One clean smack to the head almost split her head in two."

"So this one died on Saturday?"

"We're not sure how long she was dead before the body was discovered. It may have been a couple of days—give or take. That makes Wednesday the twentieth or Thursday the twenty-first the day she died."

I went over my notes and was thinking out loud. "So, we have killings on a Tuesday, a Wednesday, a Thursday and another most likely on a Wednesday or Thursday—killed in a motel room, one at home, and a phone booth on the street. How about the last one? Where did she die?"

When I paused, Dennis said, "In the middle of a building being demolished. A front-loader was about to clear debris when the driver spotted her. The body was between two walls, an exterior brick and a typical interior wall. Don't know why there was an eighteen-inch space between them, but that's where we found her body."

"I think we can rule out the first two. My first postcard coin-cided with the man who was shot," I said. "He sure likes the middle of the week. What sort of forensics did you find on this last one?"

"Nothing. Another one that seems to be the work of a pro."

We switched the conversation to more enjoyable subjects, among them, when we could get together again. The follow-ing Saturday was the first open date for Dennis. I would have preferred something sooner, but I've learned that dating a police detective doesn't provide much choice.

Later that afternoon, I covered the notes with Aaron and Effie. We made little sense of them beyond our guess about the guy who was shot while he was making a call. The Lizzy Borden reference left us cold.

14

ON MONDAY MORNING ROMEO STOOD OUTSIDE THE building where he knew Casey worked. The soothing sound of a steady drizzle did little to assuage his foul mood. His damp clothes felt like a soggy cocoon. Keeping his hands inside the outer clothing, he maintained a constant state of arousal by rubbing himself.

Due to the weather, he was unable to get close to Casey on her way to work today and he cursed the rain. He wanted to be near her. He needed to see the smile of appreciation on her face for his latest offering—a gift he so wanted her to enjoy. He thought back to last Thursday when he brought the ax down with such force it almost split the woman's head in two. He lodged her body between the plaster wall and the one made of brick. Using debris from the site, he propped her upright. Two five-foot boards made perfect crutches.

After staging the murder scene, Romeo returned to his office where he removed his outer garments—surgical scrubs, a cap and booties. He added every stitch of the other clothes he wore—shirt, pants, socks, underwear and shoes to the pile. He smiled as he watched the potential evidence being reduced to nothingness.

I'm invincible, he thought. Two murders, two M.O.s—first the gun, now the ax. The cops will never tie me to these deaths. Which M.O. will I use next? A twisted smile returned as he decided on details of the next victim's demise. Later, he disassembled the ax and dropped it into the river in different locations.

Years ago, Romeo took a creative writing course. One of the exercises was to write about a significant point in his life. This is the first person essay he wrote.

I was born at the end of the Vietnam era in 1971. That conflict held no interest for me. Many define themselves by that war, but I knew no one who served—nor did I care.

I do not remember any relatives other than my parents, Lucille and Kevin, who were too busy making millionaires out of whiskey distillers to discuss family. Their claim to fame was chugging bottles of cheap rot-gut and passing out. My parents, especially Father, liked to get an early start on the weekend, seldom waiting for Friday.

Mother usually went first, a mystery novel on her lap, slumping on the couch snoring. My father lasted long enough to whale on me for some perceived infraction of the rules. Rules, I might add, most of which were never explained to me. This was the only time he was religious—muttering his version of Proverbs 13:24, "He that spareth his rod, hateth his son…" Based on that, he did not hate me, but I could never associate beatings with love.

Father was an itinerant short-order cook. Before he became a drunk, my father was a high school English teacher. Poor speech and grammar on my part brought down his wrath and another beating. We moved a great deal, always the day before the rent came due. Packing became an art. In a half hour, my parents and I could put every-thing we owned into boxes and suitcases and stow them in the trunk of the junker car we owned. I am not sure they owned that car. My dad laughed whenever Mother mentioned a payment was due. Then, it was off to our next home where Dad would pound on me some more and Mother did nothing to protect me. How could she? She spent most of her time unconscious from booze. The one time I remember her beating me was when she walked into the bathroom and found me masturbating. She mumbled something about "spilling seed" and swatted me with the handiest item, a belt.

My only toys were the vermin that invaded our dwellings. I enjoyed kill-ing cockroaches, rats and mice—devising ever more ingenious methods of dispatching them. I left them as presents for Mother to find in the morning. An occasional stray cat or dog underwent the same fate.

I was approaching my teens when I decided I should no longer suffer being ignored nor endure any more beatings. I planned it well—it took three weeks to be sure the details were foolproof.

I needed to wait until my parents were passed out, loosen the gas connection to the kitchen range and create a timing device to set off the explosion and fire. I wanted to be far away so the police would not suspect me.

I got the idea for the timer from the movie "Stalag 17." Both my parents smoked and kept books of matches around. I tucked a lit cigarette into a match book. When the cigarette burned down far enough, it ignited the remaining matches. By the time that occurred, there was plenty of gas in the room and I could be establishing my alibi at the corner drugstore.

By the time I was thirteen, I was a millionaire. After the explosion, a shyster filed a lawsuit in my name against the slumlord who owned the building. The police arson squad ruled it an accident due to a faulty stove—two alcoholics so drunk they did not smell gas and tried to light cigarettes. No one looked at me. Why should they? I have a burn on my arm from my attempt to rescue them.

I could have come up short of a million dollars because the attorney wanted forty-percent of the settlement. It was not my size—although I was five foot ten by then—it was the look on my face and my tone of voice that convinced him. He lit

a cigarette and I told him accidents can
happen anywhere, anytime, to anyone. He
stubbed out the smoke and settled for ten
thousand dollars.

Today I still plan my activities with
the same meticulous detail. I have killed
a number of people and the police have no
clue I have been involved.

Romeo decided not to turn this piece of literature in to the
professor. He took an F for the assignment but awarded himself
an A for the insight he possessed.

He reviewed all those deaths he orchestrated over the years.
So many dead and everyone different—never the same weapon—
always a new M.O. Each involved painstaking planning, down
to the last detail.

"What can I change to throw them off?" he said. "Ah, ha. Let
us reverse the order of things." I need to get a third postcard
to Casey before I do the next deed, he thought. That meant he
would no doubt miss his window of opportunity this week and
have to wait until Thursday the following week for his next kill.
"That will give them several days to guess what and where they
should be looking."

Right now, he was doing in folks so the love of his life would
take more notice of him. He was disappointed Casey did not
show more interest—more affection for what he was doing for
her. If she did not recognize and appreciate these gifts soon, he
decided he would have to escalate his efforts and perhaps—strike
closer to home.

Rain soaked clothes were too much to bear. Romeo hurried
around the corner to his parked car. Only another ten minutes of
waiting and he would have seen Casey leave her office for lunch.

15

ON MONDAY MORNING, I DECIDED TO TAKE THE copies of the postcards to work with me. The wiper blades swooshed across the windshield. "Rain, rain, go away... I'd like to put the top down." No luck.

My plan was to contact Becca and have lunch with her. She is a mystery nut like me and has a sharp mind. I called her as soon as I arrived at my office. Becca answered with, "TrueTemp Employment Agency, how may I help you?"

I explained the reason for the call and there was excitement in her voice. "Hot damn," she said. "Trying to solve a mystery sounds like fun."

We made plans to meet at noon. I went to the office law library, pulled two volumes from the shelves and returned to my desk. My research case was interesting and it was eleven-thirty a.m. before I pulled my nose out of the books for the first time. I planned to meet Becca in a half hour, so I made a quick stop to repair my makeup and headed for the restaurant.

I arrived early and since it was no longer raining, decided to wait for Becca outside. Her British racing-green Firebird T-top roared up and screeched to a halt in front of me. She waved, shouting she would be there as soon as she found a parking slot. A squeal of tires and a pair of black rubber streaks on the pavement marked her departure. I relaxed for what I expected to be a long wait. A gal the size of Becca doesn't move too fast on land—without the Firebird, that is.

A woman came bouncing around the corner, moving at a pace that surprised me. It was Becca and it was obvious she had shed quite a number of pounds. I have only been in the TrueTemp office once in the past six months, and during that visit Becca was well-concealed behind the reception counter.

When she was close enough, I put a hand on each of her shoulders and said, "Wait a minute, gal. Let me get a good look at the new you." I took her hands, one in each of mine, and ran my eyes up and down a sleek, slim body. "How much?"

"Enough to get me down from a twenty-five to a size sixteen."

We hugged and went into the restaurant arm-in-arm.

I raised an eyebrow when she ordered.

She said, "This is my big meal of the day. It won't throw me off my diet. Let's get at them postcards." A tooth-filled smile broke out as I handed the scanned copies to her.

We talked about the past six months, my last adventure and our love lives, or lack of them. As we talked, I saw her eyes go over the copies of the cards several times. It was time to get to the business at hand. I handed her the notes I took while Dennis gave me a run down on the homicide cases he was involved in. Becca fell silent as she ate, but I could tell her mind was devouring the information on the papers she kept shuffling. I also told her what my roomies and I surmised from the info on the cards.

When she finished the papers, I said, "Okay, have you solved our mystery?"

"I think you are working too hard on the Lizzy Borden aspect. Something rings a bell with me, but I can't quite pull it up. If your assumption about the first card is correct, then we should be looking for a similar tie-in."

We talked about *The Maltese Falcon* story line. Becca threw up both hands, fell silent and I watched her eyes searching up and down and side to side. I was smart enough to keep my mouth shut.

"Casey, I remembered—if Cupid was a reference to a Sam Spade mystery, I'm wondering why."

I knocked over my water glass. "Don't keep me in suspense."

"We need the same kind of link to the Lizzy Borden clue. All we need from old Lizzy is the fact she used an ax. Dennis has a case involving an ax. The bricklayer reference is an oblique clue to the rest of the picture."

She paused while the waiter mopped the water from the table and refilled my glass. She continued, "In Dennis' ax murder, the victim was found behind a brick wall. Here's the mystery link—Edgar Allan Poe wrote a short story called *The Black Cat*. It's about this weird guy who kills his cat—gets another one and is about to kill the new one with an ax when his wife butts in. Deranged dude that he is, he whacks his wife instead of the cat. He stuffs her body behind a brick wall—ask Dennis if the body was standing up, 'cause that's how the goofball left his wife."

"Are you saying someone is killing people by imitating mystery stories?"

"That's exactly what I'm saying. What scares me most is we've got our own deranged dude and he's trying to impress you, Casey. What are you doing?"

I retrieved my cell phone from my purse and punched in Dennis' number. I expected to get his voice mail, so I was surprised when he answered. "Dennis, it's me. Was the ax victim found standing up?"

"Holy crap Casey, how the hell did you know that? That was a hold-back piece of evidence."

"It was a guess on our part, but you just confirmed it."

"What do you mean, our guess?"

I told him what Becca and I came up with. "I should say Becca, not both of us. This gal's got a sharp mind." I winked at her and she returned an appreciative smile.

Dennis said, "The victim was propped upright with a board under each arm like crutches. Casey…please… please don't breathe this to a soul. And, ask Becca to keep it quiet. I'm out on a limb again and my boss will land on my chest with both feet if he finds out I shared the details with you."

I told him he was free to share our suspicions with the other detectives. He could attribute it to the world renowned "anonymous source."

"Best hold off on that for now," he said. "Don't want my boss to think I've lost it." After a long pause, "Although…if there's a serial killer around, I wonder if we should consider your theory."

Before we ended our conversation, I checked to see if he was free on Thursday night. When I dialed again, Becca mouthed a "who." I told her I was going to update Falcon. I didn't like the idea of a serial killer stalking me either. Falcon listened without a word as I detailed our findings. He told me he was free on Thursday as well.

"What's going on Thursday night?" Becca said.

"Come over to my place about seven that evening and I'll show you."

16

WELL BEFORE DAWN ON THURSDAY MORNING, ROMEO let himself into the lobby of Casey's condo building. He felt a sexual rush when he slipped the postcard from his jacket pocket as he neared the mailboxes. Aiming the card for the slot in the door of Casey's box, he was startled as the elevator dinged to a stop on the second floor. He turned back toward the boxes and with a quick thrust put the card into the box.

Romeo realized, too late, he put the card in the wrong slot. With a string of curses trailing over his shoulder he raced for the door. Glancing back from outside, Romeo saw the lights identifying the elevator's level indicated it was going to the parking garage and knew his identity was safe.

17

I SPENT A QUIET DAY AT WORK WITH MY NOSE BURIED in law books. It was only at lunch and breaks I found myself looking forward to this Thursday evening gathering.

On my way home from work, I picked up snacks at a local deli. My next stop was a liquor store where I bought a case of beer, Chivas Regal, Margarita mix, as well as tequila and triple sec. The beer would satisfy Aaron, Dennis and Becca if she was in the mood. Chivas was Falcon's drink of choice and frozen Margaritas are good for anyone not in the mood for the other selections.

I was expecting the crowd to arrive around seven, so I was surprised when the doorbell rang at six-fifteen. I opened the door to see Kenley Longstreet standing in the hallway. Kenley is a dear same-floor neighbor. He's a self-admitted old queen with a crush on Aaron since my roomie moved in. Finding Aaron otherwise occupied, Kenley moved on to greener pastures—in the form of a gay bar not too far away named, Green Pastures. He regaled me about the place back then.

Kenley held out a hand and I saw the postcard. He said, "Looks like old Ted, the mailman, dropped this into the wrong box in the lobby." He held it up. "Your address, so it must be yours."

I thanked him and took it by the edges. He glanced at the card and said, "Sorry, I couldn't help looking at it. Rather a strange message, Casey. Anything you'd like to share?" His eyes crinkled and the mischievous smile I've seen so often appeared.

"Not right now, Kenley."

His head bobbed and he said, "Que sera, sera. Maybe some-day?" I nodded and he headed for his own door.

18

BECCA ARRIVED AT A QUARTER TO SEVEN. "I DIDN'T want to miss anything," she said.

Dennis and Falcon rang the doorbell on the dot of seven. Effie and Aaron came from their rooms. I said, "The gang's all here. Gather at the dining room table. What would you like to drink?"

Earlier I put the leaf in the table so there was plenty of room. I took drink orders and mixed a batch of frozen Margaritas. With Aaron and Effie helping, we served the crowd and got down to the business of the evening.

"Before we start, I need to tell you something," I said. "A third postcard just arrived." To a wide-eyed group, I explained the unusual delivery. "I've already made copies for everyone." I passed out the scanned copies and handed an evidence envelope out toward the guests. Both Falcon and Dennis reached for it, so I pulled it back and laid it on the table. I suggested Dennis take the head of the table and run the meeting.

Dennis said, "If you don't mind, I'll just be an onlooker. I'd rather not influence the discussions. If the conclusions are strong enough, I'll take the evidence and your theories to my bosses."

"It's your show," Falcon said, glancing at me. "Looks like you just got elected to the head slot."

Everyone took a seat and I passed out copies of the first three postcards. I gave them time to digest the images before them and take a good look at the latest arrival. "In the past, we read the cards aloud so we could soak in the information…If no one is opposed, I'll take on that chore." I looked for a head shake or a look of disapproval from the group. "Hearing no objection, let's look at my latest mail." I pointed out the address side of the card matched the first two. My hand-printed address again was almost an exact duplicate of the others. I flipped to the second scanned page. "This is where we find the differences." I read the first three lines that were printed in lower case:

```
a diller, a dollar, a ten o'clock scholar...

you used to come at one o'clock

but now you come at noon
```

I moved down to the latest image. "This time the drawing is a rectangle, bisected in the middle on the long side. One half of the rectangle is blank and the other half has five orange circles in it. Does that suggest anything to you?" I looked up from my papers and searched the eyes of everyone at the table. I also checked Dennis who was standing near the entrance to the kitchen. Falcon and Aaron began to speak at the same time, and both stopped and waved at the other.

Falcon said, "Please, go ahead, Aaron."

"It looks like a domino to me," said Aaron. "The orange dots are arranged in the same pattern found on a card or a domino. This one stands for "five. I think domino players call it an Oh – five or a "blank – five."

Falcon nodded. "You're right. The other cards didn't have color on them, did they?"

I knew his question was rhetorical, since he saw originals of the other cards. I also knew him well enough to realize he didn't ask questions without a purpose. He got the results he was looking for. Everyone began to talk at once. He held up his hands forming a T. When everyone was silent, he pointed to Effie and said, "Please go ahead."

Effie launched into her usual logical examination. "Since this is the first card with color on it, has something changed in his M.O.? Or, is the color there because it needs to be there to convey his message?" The questions hung in the air, but no one else spoke. "I thought dominos had white spots."

Falcon spoke again. "You're right. Most sets use white for the dots, but I have seen some with color. As I recall, they were larger sets that go beyond the double-six."

"Then…" Effie said. "I think the color needs to be there to figure out the riddle. So…why? What's the significance of a domino…that particular domino…and that particular color?" She stopped and waited for her observations to soak in.

Aaron looked up from his paper. "Anyone notice the nursery rhyme is mis-stated?"

I gave him a "how so" look and he continued. "I'm not sure of the exact hours used in the rhyme, but after the change the scholar comes later than usual. The verse on the card says he comes earlier."

Effie said, "Does that mean he's doing things later than normal?"

Looking at Dennis, I said, "Have there been any murders in the past couple of days—or today?"

"It's been very quiet all over town. There hasn't been a homicide since the lady was done in with an ax."

Becca leaned forward and spoke. "I think Effie's earlier question was correct—he's changed his M.O. In the past, his postcard announced a killing that was already done. Look at the rest of the message on the card." She held up her copy of the postcard and read the lines she was referring to:

```
keep your eyes peeled for late

breaking news — —
```

"Seems to me," she continued, "he's announcing the next one ahead of time. That's why his rhyme is turned around and he tells us to look to the future."

Falcon nodded in agreement and looked toward Dennis. "Does that square with you, detective?"

"It does seem a logical conclusion," Dennis said. "If he's sending forewarnings, we need to see if we can stop him. Does anyone see anything else in the message that will help?"

The group hashed out the message, over and over. Our general conclusion was the entire message referred to an upcoming event. "Let's concentrate on the drawing," I said. "What does the domino mean?"

After several minutes of some looking off into space and others muttering under their breaths, Becca slammed a flat palm on the table. Everyone stopped and waited for her to speak.

Becca looked at each of us. "The first two cards described killings that were copied from famous mystery stories." Dennis stepped forward and started to say something. Becca held up a hand. "Okay. So that's not something we know as a fact, but let's assume it's true for a minute. If this one carries on with the same theme, I've got a possible solution."

"C'mon, gal, give," I said.

"Forget the domino and concentrate on the dots—five orange dots. Ask yourself, what, besides dots, do we call those markings on dominos or dice?"

The look on Falcon's face and the slightest head nod, told me he solved the puzzle as well. He seemed to be waiting for Becca to lay it all out for us.

"If I give you the author," she said, "can you put the rest together?" Again she stopped, looking around the table. "Sir Arthur Conan Doyle."

No one said anything, but the look on Falcon's face was confirming Becca's theory.

Becca continued, "You guys should have it by now…Sherlock Holmes…The Case of…use the number and color of the dots to finish the title."

"Pips," Effie said in a voice close to a shout. "It's *The Five Orange Pips*. I know the title, but don't remember the story."

Falcon stepped in. "Holmes' client, John Openshaw, drowns."

"Great," said Dennis. "All we have to do is guard every body of water around here to prevent the next killing."

19

TOMORROW WOULD MAKE A WEEK SINCE THE meeting at my place to hash over the messages on the postcards. I was way ahead of schedule with my legal research, so my mind was wandering.

Last weekend was a general bust. Dennis called in the late afternoon on Saturday to see if I was up for dinner. I almost told him I wasn't—didn't want to seem too available. At the last minute, I relented and said yes. He explained his workload was piling up and his boss was giving him the fish-eye about the open cases on his desk. He asked if it would be all right if we met at the restaurant.

I was disappointed because I still wanted to get him into bed, and it was a month since that opportunity arose. I needed an update on his caseload since last week, so I agreed to his terms for the half-assed date he proposed.

Outside, I watched as Dennis' dusty old Ford eased into a parking slot. Months ago, I learned his nondescript police car hid an interceptor engine under the hood with lights and siren in the grill.

We embraced on the sidewalk and went inside. All through the meal, my mind drifted and I imagined myself in my bedroom with Dennis. It was a replay of the night we came the closest to… what were the kids calling sexual encounters these days? In my reverie, my cat PK was snapping a rubber band—

"Casey? Earth to Casey," Dennis said.

My image of a naked Dennis evaporated. Looking across, he was snapping his fingers. I brought us back to his job. "Have there been any murders since last week?"

He told me no and that was unusual. "More often than not, we have at least one death a week. Since the score's zero, our guy hasn't struck again.

"Did you present our theory to your boss? I mean about the postcards?"

"Yeah, and I almost got laughed out of the department. My lieutenant, Hank Oliver, was ready to put me in a rubber room when Sergeant Garrison rode to the rescue. He's been to the FBI's basic course for profilers at Quantico, and he said the postcards made sense and the guy who sent them could be a stalker."

My ears perked up and I put my fork down.

Dennis went on saying our guy didn't display the consummate definition of a stalker, but his actions were consistent with one. "Bert, Sergeant Garrison, said something about our guy fitting the 'love-obsession' stalker category, but leaving bodies for you perplexed him. Leaving gifts isn't a usual part of a stalker's scenario."

"You mean your department is looking at our ideas as a credible theory?"

"I wouldn't go quite that far." Dennis leaned over the table and spoke in a voice so soft, I strained to hear him. "But, if a drowning Vic shows up in the next couple of days...Lieutenant Oliver will probably want to interview you in person."

"I suppose that's flattering in a weird sort of way," I said.

Dennis leaned forward again and in the same low voice said, "What bothers me the most is Garrison's warning. He says if a stalker doesn't get the recognition he wants—whatever it is—he tends to escalate his actions."

I didn't find that the least bit flattering and looked around for my Hispanic guardian. I spotted de Jesus a couple of times this week, but I didn't see him anywhere tonight.

The rest of our date was as dull as his caseload report. Back outside, he pecked me on the cheek, climbed into his car and left me standing on the sidewalk.

* * *

On Wednesday morning, I was flipping through pages in the law book I was researching and made a few more notes. The clock said "coffee time," so I grabbed my cup and headed for the break room. I talked with Gretchen Love, our for-real paralegal, while I filled my mug. "Any word from the Peligrier Agency? Is Falcon going to make an appearance this week?"

Gretchen raised her eyebrows and grinned. "Do I detect more than a passing interest in the man in black?"

I did a valley-girl type head shake and shrugged.

Her grin turned into a broad smile and she said, "You know what they say about company inkwells, don't you?"

I protested. "He doesn't work for our company. He should be fair game."

Gretchen said, "You go, girl." Then she spun on her heels and headed back toward her office.

A few minutes later, back at my desk Tracy Marston rang me on the intercom and said, "Someone from Peligrier is here to see you." I hung up and started for the front of the office without responding to her. Rounding the corner to the reception area, I was sure Tracy could see the disappointment on my face. It wasn't Falcon. It was the owner's son, Vince. I saw her stifle a grin, so I said, "Have you been talking to Gretchen?" She smiled and nodded.

I realized I was in the middle of a major faux pas. At this point, there was no way to withdraw with any grace. I would have to spend time with him. He was returning an investigative report on work they did for our law firm. "Shouldn't that go to Mr. Sinclair or Mr. Westland?" I said.

"I suppose, but I'd rather give it to you. You can pass it on to the right person, can't you?"

The feeling I get every time I see Vince was dancing up and down my spine. I took the envelope and kept my comments as vague and inane as possible as I made my way back to my desk. Vince seemed incapable of picking up on social cues and followed me like a shadow. Exasperated, I told him I needed to get my work done, turned my back on him and buried my nose in a law book on my desk. I kept sneaking peeks over my shoulder without turning my head. Nothing fazed the man. He continued to sit behind me in silence. After an hour, I reached the breaking point. "Vince," I said, "I wish you would finish your business and leave." He jumped to his feet and headed toward the exit at a brisk pace.

At eleven-thirty, on my way to lunch, I dialed Dennis' number. To my surprise he answered on the second ring. I asked him if there was anything new since last Saturday night.

He told me there were no new murders in the city. Then he added, "If our guesses are correct, he'll hit again tomorrow—his usual Thursday."

I needed fresh air, so I ignored my brown bag lunch in the office fridge and headed to the mall. Entering the food court area, I noticed Raphael de Jesus. He varied his position with relation to me but kept pace with me about ten feet to my left. I stopped, trying to pick which ethnic fare to choose. Someone put a hand on my arm and said, "Chinese again, Casey?"

When I turned, I saw Gene Morse. I could also see Raphael moving at high speed in my direction. I did the most surreptitious head shake I could muster and saw Raphael's pace slow. I looked up at Gene and said, "No. I think it's Italian today."

He asked if I minded sharing a table with him and I said no. We each got a meal and met on the far side of the eating area from the food service. He set a bag on the table and said, "Remember the last time we met here?" When I nodded, he continued, "I finally got around to trying on the shirt I bought that day. It did not fit and I am returning it."

Raphael sat two tables away with a cup—coffee, I assumed— in front of him. Gene inquired about my work and asked if I was still involved with somebody. I told him I was and he said, "So I guess there is no chance you would accept an invitation to dinner." I shook my head and he changed the subject back to my work at the law firm. We chatted all the way through lunch, and then he picked up his trash and the bag. "I better return this shirt." Without another word, he headed toward the stairs to the upper levels.

Again, I thought, I never get anything out of him. He's too busy asking about me. I suppose if my relationship with Dennis doesn't pan out, he could be in the running. After another minute of thought, I decided Gene would more than likely be in line behind Falcon.

20

ROMEO WAS ANGRY. IT WAS TWO WEEKS SINCE HE axed the lady. He did not like waiting this length of time and wanted to deliver a present to Casey each week if possible.

He was also more cautious than usual. Since he sent the last postcard ahead of time rather than postmortem, he was concerned about being observed. The police are apt to be more vigilant tonight, he thought.

Romeo wondered if they linked the killings to Thursdays yet. That day fit his schedule. It coincided with the day of the week when he could use his business to help dispose of any combustible evidence. For metal, like the gun he used on the man in the phone booth, there was always an acid bath and a final resting place in the river.

From his study of criminology, he was aware of Dr. Locard's theory. In 1910 the good doctor postulated whenever two objects come into contact, a transfer of material will occur. Many criminals are tripped-up and trapped by such a transfer. Romeo theorized that if all the evidence transferred to him was obliterated, it made little difference what the police found. As far as what he left behind, if all he wore was destroyed as well, there was no chance the police could trace anything back to him. Romeo reasoned he was living proof the theory could be defeated. For this reason, he shaved his entire body precluding any transfer of his hair and his DNA to the crime scene. Two separate layers of clothing would trap anything from the killing scene or the victim. An acid bath and the all consuming flames took care of the rest. Romeo even recycled the ash that was the residue of evidence.

Unless they could catch him red-handed, he could go on forever. He prided himself on the minute details that went into his planning. Like tonight, the victim lured to this remote site at the Murray Lake section of the Arkansas River by an anonymous phone call. During his research, he learned enough about the man to make the call seem plausible. Glancing at his watch, Romeo noted it was thirty-two minutes past the agreed upon meeting time. He used the time to scan the area around the victim waiting at the end of a short pier.

Satisfied no one was watching his intended target, Romeo extracted an object from his pocket and also retrieved a smooth rock from the same pocket. He swung the object in a circle—whish…whish…whish—and released the stone. His practice with this type of slingshot paid off, and the missile struck the victim in the back of the head and he pitched into the water.

Romeo waited for ten minutes to make sure the man did not surface. No more bubbles, no sounds—he was satisfied the man was no longer breathing.

He left the scene and dropped the stolen car six blocks from where he earlier parked his own car. On the way to his business, he marveled at how little potential evidence he would need to destroy tonight—clothing and the bits of leather from his weapon would disappear in minutes.

Romeo smiled and got out a new postcard. It is time to send another one to Casey, he thought. It is time to plan for her next present. If this one does not please her, I will need to take it to her. In the words of some TV guy, up close and personal.

21

END OF THE WEEK AND DENNIS DIDN'T CALL. WE
were expecting the Thursday ritual to repeat itself yesterday.
By midafternoon, I couldn't wait any longer and dialed Dennis'
office number. When he came on the line, I said, "Well, got
anything?"

"We may have something, but I can't go into detail. Would
it mean anything if I said a couple of fishermen discovered
this one?"

"Yes, and it sounds like our best guesses just proved correct
on the location. Were we right about the date?"

"Looks like this one's been soaking for at least a day. I'd say
you were correct."

Not wanting to pass up an opportunity, I said, "How about
dinner this weekend?"

"I'd love to, but with a new open case on my desk, the boss'll
flip if I take the time off."

His voice trailed off and I hoped it was because he was disappointed. We talked for a few more minutes, and then Dennis
cut it short saying Lieutenant Oliver was on the prowl.

The rest of the afternoon dragged. I was anxious to get home
tonight, kick back and share the day's news with Aaron and
Effie. Though I didn't have many details, I was looking forward
to local TV news filling in some of the particulars.

I put my research books back in the law library and was ready
to leave at five on the dot. In the parking garage, I approached
my Mustang with key out and noticed a dark SUV parked close
to my car. I was wondering if I had room to squeeze into the

driver's door when a figure stepped from behind a concrete pillar. I had seconds to look him over before he spun me around and wrapped me in his arms. In my mind, I repeated everything I saw to imprint the detail into my gray cells. Green scrubs pulled over a black outfit, maybe a jumpsuit. Rubber gloves and a surgical hair cap. Face covered with a clear plastic mask. Looked clear, but can't discern features. Even with the head covering, I could tell he was bald.

He was dragging me toward the left side of the SUV, whispering, "Do not struggle and everything will be all right."

The mask muffled and distorted his voice. It sounded familiar, but I couldn't be sure. I twisted my head looking for an opportunity to break free.

"Let go of her," a voice with a thick Hispanic accent said.

I saw Raphael de Jesus standing five feet to our left and he was moving toward us. When he was within arm's length, my attacker slid one arm up around my neck, choking off my air. His other hand swung free and up, and he was holding a TV remote control. There are no damn TVs around here, I thought, gasping for a breath.

He pressed the remote to Raphael's neck. There was a sizzling, crackling sound and I realized what the TV remote was. Raphael collapsed to the garage floor. The man behind me pressed the Taser type stun gun to my neck and said, "See how easy that was? You want to get in on your own or do I have to lift your limp body?" He pushed me to the driver's door of the SUV, and I reached for the handle. "That is more like it, Casey. Now climb in and slide over to the right seat."

I tried to look back at him, but he told me to keep my head down and close my eyes. I did as I was told. Then, I opened my right eye—maybe I can sneak a look at him. Or, at least keep track of where he's taking me. I studied the right side door and identified the door handle and the lock button. As I thought about jumping to safety, my abductor said, "Keep your head down."

A couple of jogs and he swung a hard right turn and we accelerated. I figured we were going forty and were southbound on University Avenue. I reviewed the PLF in my mind. During my eight years with Jarvis, I took a parachute jump course and they taught me the Parachute Landing Fall—feet, calf, thigh… Piece of cake. Of course, jumping from a vehicle moving at this speed and landing on asphalt was going to leave some marks.

He was playing traffic well and seldom slowed. I pictured the route in my mind. If he took the ramp to I-630, he could connect to any number of interstates, and we might be at highway speeds for hours.

I opened my left eye enough so I could peek through the eyelashes. I was not able to see the driver, but I confirmed our speed. He edged into the right-turn only lane and I panicked as we headed toward the I-630 ramp. If I don't get out of here now, we'll be doing sixty-plus when I try to jump. Squinting my eyes and peering over the dash, I saw a slow-moving sedan in front of us. Not only slow, but the brake lights came on as well. Bless, the idiot drivers. When my abductor hit the brakes, I did it. I hit the door lock button and jerked the door handle. Pivoting ninety-degrees in my seat, I shoved the door open, planted both feet on the bottom of the door frame and propelled myself into space. Piece of cake, I thought. Then I hit and rolled.

Lack of rain in recent days conspired against me. The ground was hard as concrete and grass was so sparse there was little danger of green stains on my clothing. The piece of cake I hoped for felt more like a hard-rock candy mountain. I hit my left shoulder and felt searing pain radiate throughout my body. I raised my head enough to see the bad guy and his SUV accelerating westbound on I-630. I heaved a sigh of relief; he wasn't stopping and coming back for me. Blaring horns behind me caused me to roll over. Bad move—my shoulder gave me another shot of pain, but I saw a dark four-door climb the curbing and slow as it neared my position.

Before it stopped, I could see Raphael behind the wheel. He checked my shoulder, and over my protestations, insisted we have it looked at in an ER. For a Friday evening, the emergency room at St. Vincent Medical Center back near my office was not crowded. In the next thirty minutes, a young doctor X-rayed it, popped the shoulder back into place calling it a partial dislocation. The worst of the pain went away as soon as he finished. Next he put my arm in a sling, and told me to use ice on it several times a day. He handed me a script for pain pills, saying, "Keep it more or less immobile until the middle of next week. If the pain gets worse, use the pills and come back in for another look-see"

"Is 'look-see' a technical medical term?" I said.

He smiled. "After that, you can begin some rehabilitation exercises." He gave me a chart showing what kind of workout would be effective.

Raphael escorted me out of the hospital and insisted he would drive me home. He said he could come by in the morning, pick up one of my roommates and get my Mustang back home. As he helped me into his car, I could see two angry looking red spots on the left side of his neck. "How bad does a Taser hurt?" I said as he slid behind the wheel.

"The pain's bearable. It's the inability to control the muscles that's so damn frustrating. 'Scuse my language, ma'am."

I assured him I've heard worse and said, "Then you were conscious the whole time?"

"Yes, and I apologize for not doing my job and letting that skank grab you."

"He caught us both unaware."

"It's my job to be aware and prepared for the unexpected."

I felt no amount of words would reduce his feeling of failure. We rode west, all the way to my home in silence.

22

ROMEO POUNDED THE STEERING WHEEL OF THE SUV and cursed. He accelerated down the interstate and watched the rear view and side mirrors, saw Casey hit the ground and roll, and wondered if she was injured. "Damn." His shout was to the empty car. Before he lost sight of her, a car bounced over the curb and slowed as it approached the spot where Casey was lying.

Watching for the exit west of Ray Winder Field, Romeo stayed at the speed limit. Don't want to attract any idiot cops, he thought. He exited north, doubled back on the street to the zoo and entered the parking lot for the baseball field. The area was almost empty and it was easy to spot the second of his stolen cars. Romeo pulled into the slot facing the blue Chevrolet two-door he parked here early this morning. He sat in this first stolen car, the SUV, and looked around the parking lot. No one in sight, so he decided to remove the face mask he wore. He dropped the keys to the SUV on the seat and got out the driver's door.

Climbing into the Chevrolet, he cranked the engine and drove out of the lot. Instead of returning to the interstate, he headed north to Markham Street, then west toward Arkansas 10. In the Woodland Heights area, he maneuvered down backstreets to the place where he left his own vehicle. Again, dropping the keys of the stolen car, he looked around to be sure nothing was left behind. He kept his head turning, checking for anyone who might have an interest in him. As usual, he was away clean. Romeo was more comfortable driving his personal car and there was time to think about the recent events.

He again pounded the wheel and cursed Casey. "Why did

she act that way? I do everything to please her, and she treats me like a leper."

Romeo returned to his business and destroyed all the clothing he wore today. As he thought about Casey, a tear ran down his cheek, but it was not for Casey—it was for himself. He was wounded by her actions and was already planning his next move. He didn't think Casey would enjoy the next trip.

23

LAST NIGHT, I TOLD EFFIE AND AARON ABOUT THE latest murder. They were more interested in my adventure with the person we assumed was our mysterious murderer. I was required to tell the story three times.

This morning, I am feeling the results of my leap from the moving SUV. Somewhere in my body there must be a bone or muscle that doesn't ache. I was unable to identify it as yet. I got up early, went to the kitchen and tried to find a comfortable position to sit while my roomies fussed over me.

News travels fast. Dennis called as we were eating breakfast. "How did you hear about me?" I said.

"I got it from two sources. You can't jump out of a moving car on the interstate and not have someone report it to the police. Raphael passed the story to Falcon and he called me last night."

"Aren't you going to ask me how I feel?"

"I also got the story from the ER doc, so I know nothing's broken. Beyond that, my best guess is you feel lousy and sore all over," he said.

"You got that right. Now say something to make me feel better."

"Lieutenant Oliver wants to talk to you. Besides, you need to file a report on the kidnapping. When can you get down here?"

The doorbell rang and Aaron went to answer it. I looked at the clock on the wall and estimated the time it would take me to get into and out of the shower, then get dressed. "At the rate I'm moving," I said, "I should be ready to leave the house early next month."

"I'm serious" Dennis said. "You need to get in here today. I'll be at my desk all day. Give me a call and I'll set up the interview."

I said good-bye to Dennis, looked up and saw Falcon at the kitchen doorway. He told me he would help get my car back home. When I related what Dennis mentioned, Falcon offered to take me to police headquarters, and said, "Aaron or Effie—or both—can ride along and drive the Mustang back here."

With more bravado than I felt, I said, "I can drive."

Falcon said, "Go get ready and we'll see if you still feel that way."

It took me a little over forty-five minutes to accomplish the feat of showering and dressing. I looked at my bra and did my best to picture squirming into it. I decided this would be a bra-less day. When I was finished, I felt drained. Back in the living room I said, "I'll take anyone up on the offer to drive my car back here." Looking at Falcon, I said, "Wipe that grin off your face." He laughed out loud. So much for my commanding presence.

At the police station, Falcon insisted on sitting in with me during the interview with Lieutenant Oliver. The lieutenant asked him if he was an attorney and when Falcon shook his head, Oliver said it wasn't possible for him to be in the interview room.

Falcon said, "Is she a suspect in any investigation or is she under arrest?" When Oliver said no, Falcon continued. "Either I sit in as an advisor, or we're out of here."

The three of us sat down in a small drab interview room, which contained the obligatory wall mirror. Even though I wasn't a suspect, the whole scene was intimidating and I wondered who was watching through what I assumed was a two-way mirror—or are they called a one-way mirror? I never understood the term.

Lieutenant Oliver was good at the process and put me at ease almost at once. He said, "Tell me what's been happening?" I began talking and during the next half hour he needed to ask only two questions to keep me going. "…and that's when I jumped out of the guy's SUV," I said, wrapping up my story.

Oliver smiled. "Good job, Ms. Fremont. That's quite a story. If it wasn't for Dennis, Detective Epstein, and the fact you helped us on the double murder last fall, I'd dismiss your allegations out of hand. I think you'd have to agree, on the face of it—it seems farfetched."

I didn't say anything and he continued. "I mean, a guy you don't know, kills people and sends you postcards announcing the murders."

"I didn't say I didn't know him," I said.

"You mean you know who it is?"

"No. I mean I can't imagine a perfect stranger doing this."

"Don't discount strangers," Oliver said. "You may remember the case of Rebecca Schaeffer, the TV actress? That killer sent her all kinds of notes and letters, but didn't know her or meet her until the day he murdered her."

I did my best to take the strain off my aching shoulder by resting the forearm on the gray steel table. Not much help. "Oh, great. Now I have to worry about every nutcase on the planet as the possible stalker."

Oliver leaned toward Falcon and me. "I'm going to put a surveillance team on you, at least part-time. They will be using a video camera and we can review the tapes to see if the same face shows up."

Falcon briefed Oliver on Raphael de Jesus. "I'd hate for your guys to mistake him for the stalker."

"Appreciate the heads up," Oliver said. "I wish you'd pull him out of the equation." When Falcon gave him a frowning head shake, Oliver continued, "At least provide us with a photo."

Falcon flipped open a notepad portfolio, pulled out a picture and slid it across the table toward the lieutenant. "If that's all, we need to pick up Ms. Fremont's car and get her back home."

"Wait a minute, you two," I said. "You're talking here like I don't exist." Both the men turned toward me. "Now...I've got some questions. Lieutenant Oliver, does this mean you believe our theory of the murders?"

"Well, that is one of several leads we're pursuing."

Falcon held up a hand. "That's funny. I hear you got zilch in the way of motives or evidence—"

"Where did you hear that?" Oliver said.

"The chief of police is on my payroll," Falcon said. Oliver did a double take and Falcon said, "You know I'm not going to give up sources, so don't bother asking. You can continue to stonewall or you can share. You share; I share."

With a shrug that showed his reluctance, he said, "You've got it pretty much right. There has been no traceable forensic evidence at the crime scenes. As for motive, that's thin too. Other than trying to impress Ms. Fremont, we don't see one. He appears to be a stalker who kills." Oliver opened the case folder and riffled pages. "That's about it. I'd appreciate it if you keep this information confidential. Now, what do you have?"

I shook my head and Falcon said, "What I've got, you know."

We both stood to leave and Oliver said, "Sit down. I'm not through yet."

24

I STARTED TO OBJECT TO OLIVER'S DEMAND THAT WE remain in the interrogation room. He looked toward the wall mirror and waved an arm like he was inviting someone to enter.

In a few seconds the door to our room opened and a head appeared. "Garrison, come on in," Oliver said. He looked at me and Falcon. "This is Sergeant Norbert Garrison, our profiler. Norbie, go ahead and fill these two in on our ideas about the stalker-killer."

Garrison dragged a chair from a corner to the table, making a grating sound as the chair legs resisted against the bare floor. "This guy may cause the experts to add a new chapter to a book on stalkers. In many respects, he's a textbook 'love-obsession' type of stalker. But…"

He got me to bite. "But, what? I'm not sure I like being the object of a new breed of weirdo." I slid my forearm off the table. When it jerked to a stop at the end of the sling, I flinched. It felt like taking my lower lip and pulling it up over my forehead. I looked at Falcon, who seemed intent on staring a hole in the wall, high up in a corner.

Garrison scooted his chair closer to the table. "Communicating, albeit postcards versus letters, is a classic trait. Other ways he fits the pattern is actual stalking. I think we have to assume he's out there watching you. When he didn't get whatever it was he fantasized about, he introduced threatening behavior when he abducted you."

He paused his narration and waited to see if I had anything to say. All I felt was a shiver up and down my spine.

Garrison continued. "Beyond those, the guy's like a derailed train—not following the pattern. He keeps his identity concealed. He kills people and tells you about them. It's like he's leaving presents for you—trying to impress you."

Garrison paused again and looked around the table at the three of us. "Although he could be a total stranger, my hunch is he's someone you know, Ms. Fremont. Could be a casual and brief meeting. As long as they get what they consider encouragement, they tend to continue on a somewhat even keel. A classic case was that TV actress—Rebecca Schaeffer—who was killed in 1989."

I nodded and said, "Lieutenant Oliver mentioned her too."

"Yes, she's a good example of what stalkers can do. Anyway, her killer sent her fan mail and her reply closed with the word 'love' and that was enough for him to continue and intensify his fantasy." He stopped and stared at me.

"I can't imagine anyone I know could be doing this," I said. "You indicated they can continue on a rather even keel for a while. What causes them to escalate?"

"I'll use the Schaeffer case as the example again," Garrison said. "She did a love scene in a movie; he saw it and that set him off and he decided to kill her."

"What if I don't do anything to set him off? Will he eventually stop?"

"They never stop. I'm not sure what happened in your case, but our guy stepped up his obsession by abducting you. He thinks you've already rebuffed him—at least in his own mind."

"What did I do?" I said.

Garrison leaned back in his chair and shook his head. "He came, dragged you off to take you…somewhere. And, you jumped out of his car. That's going to be a major rejection to him."

"What would he have done if I went with him?"

Garrison said, "I don't know. But I wouldn't put any money on a positive outcome. I think he's about to the end of his tether. He's ready to escalate his actions against you."

The interrogation room door opened and Dennis stuck his head in. "Boss. A blue and white reported spotting the SUV used in Casey's…Ms. Fremont's kidnapping."

25

LIEUTENANT OLIVER WAVED A HAND SUGGESTING we should follow him. He was busy questioning Dennis as we trailed after the pair to a communications room. He and Dennis entered the small area. Falcon, Sergeant Garrison and I crowded into the doorway trying to hear what was going on out in the field. The lieutenant donned a headset with a boom mike and began a series of rapid-fire questions. He hit a switch on the console and the speakers went dead. Now, we heard only one side of the discussions. I got the feeling Oliver was talking on both the police radio and a landline phone. After a few minutes, he slammed his headset down.

"Damnit," Oliver said. "The uniforms at the scene ran the plates on the SUV. It was reported stolen two days ago. Our UNSUB must have stashed another car in the parking lot at Ray Winder Field."

I racked my brain. UNSUB? I knew that acronym from somewhere, but I couldn't remember the meaning.

"Unidentified Subject," Falcon said in a quiet tone in my ear.

I looked at him. "How the hell do you do that?"

"Body language and a lot of luck," he said.

I punched his arm. "Quit grinning."

Lieutenant Oliver pushed his way through the throng saying, "Looks like the crime scene will be as bare as the rest."

The words trailed over his shoulder as he moved at a brisk pace away from us. Not seeing a signal to follow, we waited to ask Dennis the questions running around in our heads.

Dennis relayed the other side of the communications to us. Nothing in the car appeared to be left behind by our suspect.

A Crime Scene Search Unit which was returning from another assignment is already processing the SUV. Initial report looked dismal. No fingerprints, no nothing. They would impound the vehicle and bring it in for further examination…but no one seemed to be holding his breath.

26

I SPENT MOST OF SUNDAY RESTING. BETWEEN NAPS
and the pain pills the ER doc gave me, I was feeling decent
most of the time. When I decided on a shower, another problem
cropped up. Not wanting to get my sling wet, I took it off and
lowered my left arm. Mistake—big mistake. The pain in my
shoulder brought me up short. I bent my elbow and supported
the arm with my other hand. All I have to do is take a no-hands
shower. I took a deep breath…and screamed for help.

Effie ran into my bedroom with a look a panic on her face.
"What's wrong, Casey?"

I explained the situation and she grabbed a roll of gauze from
the bathroom vanity and fashioned a sling. "I'll make a couple
of extras," she said. "Then you won't have to yell for help."

I realized how self-centered I was becoming. "I'm sorry."

Even with the improvised support for my left arm, I found
it difficult to finish my shower. I was amazed at how many
automated rituals I incorporate into my routine. I figured about
sixty-five percent of me was clean when I gave up and turned
off the water. Drying my body was as tough as washing…and
dressing was going to be an equal challenge. Looking at the
clothes laid out on the bed, I knew getting them on would be
a test of skill. My panties were up to my hips with a minimum
of twists. Eyeing the bra, I knew I was again facing an impossible task.

I can get along without a bra today, but that's putting off the
inevitable. I picked it up and stabbed my good arm through a
strap and it hung from one shoulder. Past that, I had no idea
what the next move would be.

I poked my head through the bedroom door and called Effie.

"Her door is closed and I can hear the sewing machine," Aaron said. "Can I help?"

I shrank behind the door. From the sound of his voice, there was no more than fifteen seconds before a decision would have to be made. I needed help and he wasn't after my body. Other men have seen me nearly naked. I'm the landlord and he's a tenant. Oh, what the hell does that have to do with anything?

Poking my head back through the cracked door, I said, "I need help getting my bra on and hooked. I've only got panties on."

"If it's not a problem for you, it's not a problem for me."

I retreated into the room, turned my back to the door and said, "Come in."

Aaron entered and over my shoulder I could see him survey-ing my predicament—the slightest smile on his lips. He seemed more familiar with the intricacies of brassieres than I would have expected. With everything arranged and in its proper location, he fastened the hooks and eyes on the back.

"Tight enough?" he said. When I nodded, he added, "Any-thing else I can do?"

I shook my head and he told me he'd see me in the living room. My bedroom door closed with a click. I managed a pair of baggy sweat shorts, a T-shirt and a pair of flip-flops.

Aaron's nose was buried in the sports section when I got to the living room. I hid behind the editorial part of the paper.

"Hi, everybody," Effie said as she breezed into the room. "What do you think of this dress?"

Aaron and I both grunted a reply from behind our newspaper pages and I didn't glance at the clothing she was holding. We were silent for a minute.

"That's an exciting confidence builder," Effie said. Another minute of silence. "All right, you two. What's going on?"

Aaron and I stared at each other for a few seconds, then I said, "Okay, I guess we're busted." I related the details of the Great Bra Caper to Effie.

She folded the material across one arm and sat down. She stared at us and said, "Aaron? Can I ask you a question?" Aaron said yes, and she said, "I mean a really personal question." Aaron nodded. "How did you know you were gay?"

I think the question surprised me more than it did Aaron. He didn't answer at once but looked like he was composing a response as he shifted in his seat.

"Don't think I've ever been asked that in such a direct manner." He described growing up in an area of Little Rock where he "didn't advertise his lifestyle in the hood." "By the time I reached junior college, I was darn sure of my orientation, but there was always the pressure to pray for a 'cure' for the gay.' I dated a couple of women, but even the sex wasn't satisfying." He paused for reactions. "Does that answer your question, Effie?"

"What cure?" she said.

"In my church, the Sunday sermons indicated if I put my mind to it, I could switch back to being a heterosexual. Like it was something I could turn on and off…enough about me. Effie, show us the dress again."

She rose and held it up in front of her. It looked good and we both told her so. Her studies on clothing design were paying off. "Good work, Effie," I said. "Aaron, how's your architectural course going?"

"I really should be doing some studying today," he said. He excused himself and went to his room. Effie returned to her work, and I fumed over the contents of the editorial page.

* * *

Monday, and a new workweek was beginning. I wanted to put in an appearance at my law firm.

Mr. Sinclair, a partner, was aware of my weekend ordeal. "Saw the news reports about you on TV, Casey. Glad to see you here, but don't overdo it. Take it easy until you're feeling one-hundred percent."

I thanked him and took his words as an invitation to visit the break room for coffee and a Danish. While I was there, Marcia Kavenaugh came in. We chatted for several minutes before she headed back to her office. Marcia is a firm lawyer who was passed over for partner. A younger male attorney was selected for partner in her place. I assumed those circumstances could generate a lot of animosity.

Marcia was a big woman. Not out of proportion, just large boned and big. She's darn near the size of my abductor. I picked up a flyer about a company picnic from the table. The back side was blank and I wrote "Killer-Abductor Candidates" at the top. The first name I listed was Marcia's. I used the rules of brainstorming, omitting no one and not stopping to rationalize about the entries. If they fit the size criteria, the name went on the list. When I ran out of steam, I put the pen tip on the first entry, read it and thought about the person.

"Marcia Kavenaugh." Big enough to fit the bill. No doubt ticked off at the law firm, but why would she take it out on me?

"Dennis Epstein." Wonder why I put him on the list. Police officer, almost a lover. Not really a probable suspect except he fits size wise.

"Vince Peligrier." P.I. firm; son of owner. Right size, but such a wuss. Be wary of the quiet ones I reminded myself.

"Falcon." Investigator for the Peligrier Agency. Right size, but…naaah. But…what do I really know about him?

"Gene Morse." My guardian angel from those murders last fall. He's a little peculiar, but I can't imagine him killing a flea.

"Aaron Kincaid." Right size, wrong color. I'm pretty sure I would have known if my attacker was black.

"Jarvis Parnell Sheffield, the Third." My ex. Sure glad I went back to my maiden name. I slept with the idiot for years; can't imagine him as a killer. Although, he did threaten violence if I didn't get back together with him.

"Question Marks." Some unknown nutcase.

That was the last entry on my list and I was no closer to an answer than when I started—I looked at my watch—forty-five minutes ago. Oops. Not sure Mr. Sinclair meant to take this much time on breaks. I'm positive—well almost positive my abductor was bald. Everyone on the list had a full head of hair. I suppose someone who is bald or has a shaved head could invest in an expensive toupee.

Enough detective work for one day, I thought. I went back to my desk and picked up the research I was working on last Friday.

Later the same day, I was absorbed in the task when a voice behind me said, "Hi, Casey."

I recognized the voice. Without turning I said, "Hello, Vince. What are you doing here?" He moved to the side of my desk and did what I've come to think of as the Vince Shuffle—somewhere between St. Vitas dance and a full-body tic.

"I heard about your ordeal over the weekend. I wanted to see if you're okay."

Using my right hand to lift the left one, I winced and said, "Not too bad. All things considered, it could have been worse. I could have broken something."

Does it still hurt?"

I felt like clubbing him, but settled for a head nod. As he launched into one of his patented soliloquies, I thought of my morning activity and the list of possible bad guys. I found myself staring at his hair.

His hands shot up. "Is there something wrong with my head?"

"No, Vince. You're fine. Please go on with your story."

I tore my eyes from him. Paying no attention to his words, I concentrated on thinking about hair—or lack of hair? I've seen so many bad toups which are easy to spot. I wondered if I could detect a really good one. An expensive one. I decided I could. That was a gut feeling but my logic was battling with this opinion.

Vince turned in his chair and appeared to be focusing on something beyond my left shoulder. I scrutinized his hairline from forehead to sideburn and over his left ear.

"Keep talking, Vince. I need a book from the next desk and I'll still be able to hear you." Without changing position, he continued his one-sided conversation and I circled him. I was able to examine the right side of his head as well as the hairline on the nape of his neck.

I returned carrying a law book I didn't need. I sat down and felt foolish for examining Vince's head. One thing's for certain. Vince does *not* wear a toupee. At least, I don't think he does.

27

ON MONDAY MORNING, ROMEO SCANNED THE newspaper at a nearby cafe. There was nothing in the paper yesterday, and he was still looking for a story about Casey. He wondered why the story about his kidnapping her was almost nonexistent. A small blurb on page A-19—the next to the last page in the first section—mentioned a woman jumping from a vehicle on I-630—no name, no details. He pondered the reasons the police would protect…cover up and not release the particulars.

With a disgusted shrug, Romeo tossed the paper onto the next table and concentrated on his coffee and plans for Casey. He took deep breaths to regulate his breathing and calm himself. He was angry, mad…irate that Casey escaped last Friday. She spoiled a good weekend. Romeo tore his thoughts away from the images of his plans for her over the past couple of days.

His intellect, slowed to its usual methodical pace, began reviewing his next moves. He looked around to be sure no one else was sitting in this corner of the coffee shop. "This must be an astounding event. A grand finale. The culmination of our relationship—Casey's and mine. I will invite the police, everyone, to witness this last death. This week the fat lady will sing."

Another cup of coffee and he was on the third page of the small notepad he always carried. The message for the postcard was roughed out. Romeo constructed a simple substitution cipher and encoded the clue to the location. He was pleased with his progress. "I think I will need to see Casey this week."

He ordered a final cup of coffee and a sandwich, which he wolfed down. Decisions made, Romeo was eager to put his plans in motion. He packed up his belongings, looked around to be sure nothing was left behind and walked out into the bright sunshine.

28

BEFORE LEAVING WORK, I CALLED BECCA AT
TrueTemp and invited her to my place for dinner. I wanted input
on the postcards and what we knew about the murders…and
what we didn't know.

She begged off because of a date, so we settled on the next
day. "See you tomorrow," I said.

* * *

On Tuesday, getting dressed became easier. As of today, it was
a one-woman job. When I made the announcement at breakfast, it brought a smile from Aaron. At work, I did have trouble
lugging reference books to my desk and found it difficult to
concentrate on my work. Thinking about tonight, I was eager
to sit down with Effie and Becca and our postcards. Aaron was
on a two-day trip and would miss our talk. Since my research
work was suffering anyway, an early lunch served as a diversion.
Driving was still a chore—walking to the nearby mall was the
easiest answer.

On the escalator down to the food court area, a voice behind
me said, "How do you do it Casey? You must be a mind reader
to know what days to come here to meet me."

Surprised, I turned to see Gene Morse smiling at me. "Well,
I don't…I didn't…I mean…Okay, you caught me."

We chatted and I was about to invite him to join me, when
he said, "I would love to have lunch, but I need to get going.
Got a client waiting." With a quick wave and a smile over his

shoulder, he disappeared toward the exit to the parking garage. I was checking over the possible lunch choices when I spied another man I know. It was Falcon. I started toward him and he retreated. That brought a frown to my face. What the hell's the matter with him? I know he saw me. I pulled out my cell and dialed his portable. He turned his back, answered his phone and said, "I know you see me. Just go about your business so I can do my job."

"What damn job?" I said.

"Keeping an eye on you. Raphael is busy on another assignment today. Good-bye."

I could see him stab the END button on his cell and start for the other side of the room. "Okay, then…screw you," I said to a dead connection.

I ate and walked back to my office. There was a pink message slip on my desk. I returned the call from Dennis and he asked me out tonight. I begged off, not telling him about my who-dunnit meeting with Becca and Effie. My excuse was lame, but I didn't want him there. I was looking for non-police input, and he was too involved with his job.

My law research was progressing well when I was interrupted in the middle of the afternoon. I looked up from my desk and saw two men standing there. Falcon was quiet as usual…and as usual Vince was into his full-body tic. Standing behind Vince, Falcon was shaking his head. I made an "eating" motion with my hand and gave him a pair of arched eyebrows. He shook his head again, so I made no mention of our luncheon encounter. Turned out, Vince was here to deliver some information from his daddy's PI firm that I was waiting for, and Falcon said he "tagged along." I knew that must be a lie. I decided long ago, Falcon never does anything by accident.

This has been a weird day, I thought.

* * *

At six p.m., Effie and I were busy in the kitchen. That's the royal "we," since I needed to dance to stay out of her way. She was finishing three grilled chicken breasts which would be sliced for a salad topping. The doorbell rang.

"Becca's early," I said and left the kitchen.

Peering through the front door peephole, I let out a sigh loud enough for Effie to hear. In response to her call, I said, "No problem. It's just Jarvis the Rat." I could hear her giggling; I opened the door and tried to block it with my foot. Jarvis was pushing hard and my left shoulder was toward him. No contest. He won the shoving match.

"Damnit, Casey, I left three voice mails for you today. Why didn't you call back?"

"Why do you suppose I did that?" Then I shut up. Fuming and shifting his weight from one foot to the other, he tried to step around me and get to the living room. I sidestepped and blocked his progress. He feinted left and tried to go right. I blocked him again. His face and body language gave him away. I could see the frustration building.

"If you don't take me back, I don't know what I'll do next."

"Jarvis…Jarvis, listen to me." I put a hand on each of his shoulders. Considering the pain in my left arm, I hoped he appreciated the effort. "Here's what you're going to do next." I explained there was no "us" anymore—there wouldn't be an "us" in the future—and if he didn't get professional help, I'd get a restraining order against him. "And that's why I didn't return your calls."

Letting my hands drop from his shoulders, I stepped back. "Do you understand what I'm saying?"

Jarvis looked like his body received an injection from a giant needle full of Novocain. Shoulders slumping, he nodded and mumbled "yes" in a weak voice. He let me ease him out the door. I looked through the peephole and watched him slouch down the hall. He turned, shook a fist at my door then punched the elevator button. The door opened. Jarvis disappeared and Becca stepped out of the elevator.

I ushered Becca into the kitchen and covered Jarvis' visit with her and Effie. I went to the computer room while Effie served our dinner. I put copies of our three postcards, my list of "probables" and the notes we gathered from our police visits on the table.

We were near the end of our meal when I heard PK make his grand entry into the living room—splot. He staggered into the dining room shaking his head. I wondered when his encounters with the wall mural would begin to sink in. PK doesn't get people-food, and he's not allowed on the table, but that was his next stop. Sitting on the far end of the table from us, he gave his most pathetic meow. I retaliated with an evil-eye and a pointing finger. He flopped down on the table and rolled over waiting for a belly rub.

I know when to retreat. I scooped him up and put him on the floor as I moved to the kitchen for another bottle of wine. With full glasses, we tackled the stack of material in front of each of us.

Holding up my list of "possibles," I said, "Can you think of anyone to add?"

"Do you think the killer is on this list?" Becca said.

Effie said, "I hope so, because if he's not, we might as well add the whole Little Rock phone book."

Becca laughed. "What makes you think it couldn't be a stranger?" No one answered her. "Casey, if you were forced to choose, who would you pick?"

It took me a longtime to reach a non-decision. "I sat next to the guy in a truck and the only thing I'm sure about is he's bald."

"Are any of these guys bald?" Becca said.

"Not that I can tell," I said. "I can't even make an intelligent guess."

We all set the list aside and considered the murders. The first postcard contained a picture of Cupid and the message was related to Dashiell Hammett's *The Maltese Falcon*. The police found a man shot in a phone booth, which matched what happened to Sam Spade's partner, Miles Archer. An image of a black cat was the centerpiece on the second card. That led to *The Black Cat* by Poe pointing to a woman killed with an ax—which is what the police found. A body behind a wall with her skull split.

"Before we get to the last one," Becca said, "Have you noticed the one thing that's the same on all three?"

Effie and I pawed through our copies of the cards shaking our heads. "The images and the words are different on all three," I said.

"Look at how the messages end," Effie said.

"Exactly," Becca said. "Those two lines are repeated on all—almost like a signature."

"But what could those two marks stand for?" My question hung on the air and none of us would hazard a guess. I picked up the copy of the image of a zero-five domino. Drowning was a theme of *The Five Orange Pips* by Arthur Conan Doyle. Right on schedule, the police found the next body in a local lake. Time of death occurred on Thursday, as best they could tell. It matched the day of the week of the first two. Seems our guy likes to kill on Thursday.

"Why in the world would that be?" Effie said.

Becca said, "I've done some research on that. 'Member the old rhyme about children?" When none of us spoke, she continued. "Well, it starts 'Monday's child is fair of face'…then goes through the week and gets to 'Thursday's child has far to go'…could that relate to the first message?"

We could not tie that idea in, so we chewed on the bone and listed our guesses: day off from work, wants to get rid of the evidence the next day, anal-retentive compulsion, travels out of town on the other days …

There weren't any comic strip balloons with a light bulb enclosed over any of our heads. We moved to more important things—discussing the current bottle of wine we were draining.

29

ROMEO APPROACHED CASEY'S BUILDING WITH caution. He disliked coming so early—too easy for someone to see him—but he needed a few more hours tonight to make final arrangements for Thursday's killing. And he wanted them to have two full days to figure out his clue. Moving into the empty lobby, he tugged the mask over his face. Romeo felt a chill of excitement run up his back and in his groin.

Pulling the postcard from a jacket pocket, he slipped it into Casey's mailbox slot and turned toward the street exit. A Mexican blocked the door. I have seen this man before, he thought. He is the one who was following and protecting Casey.

Romeo's mind ticked off several scenarios, but only one made sense—kill this man—now. He slid a small caliber automatic from under the jacket, steadied the weapon with two hands and put a bullet into the man's forehead. Romeo secured the gun back in its holster, scooped up the spent shell casing from the floor and stepped over the body.

Damn. I was hoping to hang onto this pistol for a while. Now I will have to dispose of it on Friday. Good thing I have spares to use Thursday night.

Outside the building, Romeo faded into the gathering darkness and pulled off his ski mask. In minutes, he could not be identified from the other commuters on the streets.

30

THE THREE OF US WERE STILL AT THE TABLE SIPPING wine and discussing the notes I wrote about my police interviews when the doorbell rang. PK, my brave protector, took off like a streak headed for my bedroom.

The view through the peephole revealed my same-floor neighbor, Kenley Longstreet. I opened the door and he said, "Casey, there's been a shooting in the lobby. I think it's the Hispanic fellow you said was helping you."

I was speechless. Effie and Becca were standing behind me, and Effie said, "You mean Raphael?"

I nodded and so did Kenley. He said, "If you're okay, I'll get back to the lobby. I found the body and the police will no doubt want to talk to me."

Back inside my home, Becca said, "Who was that?" I told her his name and she continued, "How come he's not on your bad-guy list? He comes pretty close to fitting the description—and he wears a toupee."

"He's such a dear, sweet man. I can't imagine him hurting anyone," I said.

When I gave Becca more details about Kenley, she said, "That's too bad. He's a cutie. Wonder if he'd like to go out anyway?"

The next interruption was Dennis on the phone checking on my well-being. He was pulling up outside my building and said he would be up to see me in a half hour or so. Falcon's call came in before I could put the cordless down. When I answered, the sound of tires screaming in protest came over the phone as he spoke. I told him I was okay and he said, "How the hell did our guy get the drop on Raphael?"

"I don't know."

"I know you don't. I'm venting and thinking about his wife and kids. How the hell am I going to tell her? I'll be there in twenty minutes."

The voice and squealing tire sounds were gone. There was no use saying any more, his phone was off.

Effie said, "What was the killer doing here anyway?" She didn't wait for an answer. "I bet there's another postcard in the mailbox."

I grabbed my keys and the three of us jammed through the front door all at the same time, reminding me of the ever-present collision in sitcoms. The elevator door in the lobby opened to chaos. Crime scene-tape prevented us from taking more than one step into the lobby. The only exit was to hug the wall and make for the door leading to the parking garage. Dennis came through the front door. I yelled and waved him over. I told him we suspected there was another postcard in my mailbox.

"Okay," he said. "Let's take a look."

The three of us reached for the yellow tape, planning to duck under. "Whoa," said Dennis. "Only one of you." He pointed at me. "Be careful where you step."

A single card rested in the mailbox. I reached for it and Dennis slapped my hand aside. "That's evidence," he said. With the help of a uniformed officer, he slid the card into a clear plastic evidence envelope. He started to walk away and I said, "Wait a damn minute. Where are you taking that?" Dennis explained he would lock it in his car to protect the chain of evidence.

"Not until I scan a copy of it," I said. "You can come with me if you want—to protect your precious chain of evidence. But… that card's not leaving this building until I have a copy."

Evidence bag in hand, Dennis trailed Effie, Becca and me into the elevator and up to the eighth floor. I put the bag flat on the scanner glass, clicked the mouse button three times and waited for the scanner lamp to warm up. When the first copy was churning out of the printer, I lifted the scanner lid, flipped the evidence bag over and started the next scan. The printer coughed out the second side and I check both images to be sure they were legible.

Dennis reached over my shoulder and retrieved the envelope. "Got any ideas on this one?" He looked at the three of us as if he expected an answer.

I pointed toward my front door and said, "Don't call us. We'll call you…What do you expect? We haven't even read this one yet."

Dennis shrugged and walked out.

"Let's make extra copies of this puppy," I said. "Then we can get back to work."

31

A FRESH GLASS OF WINE AND TWO PAGES IN FRONT of each of us, we all put on a frown and stared at the newest postcard. Effie was the first to speak. "The address side is a virtual carbon-copy of the others. Do you want me to read the other side aloud?"

Hearing no objections, Effie took a sip of wine and picked up her copy of the card. "The image on this one is a white cat, curled up taking a nap. The text looks like the same font as the others. Above the cat it reads:

```
mix mexican and chinese

how can you tell a cat is radio active?"
```

She paused. "Ring a bell with anyone yet?"

"Let's hear all of it before we start guessing," I said.

Becca cocked her head and said, "Wait a minute." We watched her as she leaned back and moved her gaze around the room. "No use. I thought I was getting close to something—but no luck. Go ahead, Effie."

Effie picked up the image again. "Below the cat, it says:

```
Solve the clue in time and you can see
            me in action—

    pznenp       oziab7       bqlfdn


      6qc4li       7qp24p"
```

"That part is different from anything we've seen before," I said.

It was Becca's turn. "He says, 'solve the clue' so I bet it's encoded words…like those cryptograms in the newspaper."

"I think Becca's right," Effie said. "Either of you good at codes?"

Becca said, "No, and it's not a very big sample. Thirty characters if I counted right…Hey wait a minute. I know a lady who teaches at the Arkansas School for Mathematics, Science and the Arts in Hot Springs and—"

"Oh, that's a mouthful. But isn't that a high school?" I said.

"Yes, but the place is full of some of the sharpest kids around. I bet they have some math and computer whizzes who would love to tackle this?"

"Won't the police be working on it too?" said Effie.

"It won't hurt to have other eyes looking at it." Becca fished an address book from her purse and headed to the living room. We could hear her on the phone.

When she came back to the dining room, we turned our efforts to the message on the card. Looking at my copy, I said, "Is the message about the cat or the fact the cat is sleeping?"

"We've already seen a cat," Effie said. "The message here might be about sleeping."

Putting that part aside, we concentrated on the text. Mixing Mexicans or Hispanics with Chinese didn't make much sense. We couldn't relate it to anything that rang a bell. I wondered aloud if the reference to Mexicans could refer to Raphael de Jesus. We cataloged the idea, but set it aside as well.

Several minutes of wine sipping and mind bending followed before Becca reminded us we were looking for a mystery story. "By the way, what's the name of the instrument they use to check for radio activity?"

"Geiger counter," Effie and I said at the same time.

We pondered the name, but couldn't tie a story title to it. "Do you think the last two lines mean anything beyond what they say?" I said. Two shaking heads met my glance. "Okay, then let's concentrate on the first two lines of text. Maybe the internet will help." We packed up our wine and images and moved to the den.

As we settled in front of the computer, PK assumed his usual computing position—curled up on top of the monitor. I opened Google and typed in "sleeping cat," which returned a bunch of hits about actual images of sleeping cats. Not much help. Next, I tried "sleeping cat mysteries." Most of these returns were about books by authors who did not fit the famous type our killer seemed to like. A "mystery sleep" search revealed a little more. There were some references to *The Big Sleep*. One was a book-store in St. Louis and the other was from Amazon.com, which specified *The Big Sleep* by Raymond Chandler.

I revised my search criteria using the book name. After reviewing a couple of sites, we found some ah-ha's. The man who hires Phillip Marlow has a daughter named Carmen—possible Mexican tie-in. The victim is named Geiger—another tie-in and he is killed wearing an embroidered Chinese coat.

Effie said, "I'd say we have enough background to prove we're on the right track. Three details tie it to the name of the book."

I looked at the clock and both hands were pointing straight up. I offered Becca the other half of my bed for the night. I reminded her I owned spare toothbrushes, and she accepted. We were packing up our clues when Dennis called.

"Hi, babe," he said. I figured he was using the light and breezy approach to cover his rather cool departure earlier.

"Hi, yourself. Has the LRPD solved the latest mystery?" I heard him suck in a loud breath before he answered.

"Nope. How you doing?"

I explained we understood the book clue, but didn't know how to go about solving the encrypted part. He related the police department's position on the code. The UNSUB was playing more games with us, the message would no doubt turn out to be nothing of importance, they would not expend investigative time on it and wouldn't involve any other agencies—state, local or federal.

Those pronouncements blew my mind. "I think your department's attitude is ridiculous and stupid." He sucked in another breath, but I beat him to it. "Our UNSUB has played it straight from the git-go. He sends a clue—it proves true. Now, he invites us to a killing and you guys are going to ignore it. Like I said—stupid."

Leaping to the defense of the police department, he recited what sounded like company policy and dogma and a bit of B.S.—manpower shortages, caseloads, priorities—

"Priorities," I said at a volume I'm sure caused him to jerk the receiver away from his ear. "For craps sake. You got a serial killer running loose. What could be a higher priority?"

"We're not positive we do have a serial killer. There's no forensic evidence to link the deaths, the M.O.'s vary, and beyond several crackpot postcards, we have nothing to tie it all together." Dennis took a half-second to inhale so he could continue.

Too bad he never learned to take a breath and keep talking, I thought. My words were flowing before he could organize himself. I reiterated my ideas, pointing out the police's position was ridiculous. "No serial killer, my ass. I bet the local papers would love copies of the postcards and a few details tying the cards to the dates of the deaths."

"Casey," he said. "You wouldn't dare go to the papers. You could be charged with obstruction and interfering with a police investigation."

"I'm talking about anonymous tips. Who would you prosecute?"

"Okay. Okay. Let's start over. I understand your frustration. Don't shoot the messenger."

The temperature of the air between us warmed a few degrees. I told him about Becca's contact at the Math and Science school. He was glad to hear someone was working on the problem. We settled on a dinner date for Friday.

Dennis closed with, "See you then, unless our non-serial killer hits again on Thursday and we're wrapped around the axle by Friday."

32

THIS MORNING, I DECIDED TO FACE THE DAY WITHOUT the sling for my arm. The exercises I used, the ones the ER doc recommended, seemed to be working. I knew I wasn't back to one-hundred percent, but I was close enough—and was getting tired of lugging my arm around in that damned sling.

At work, Wednesday dragged like a half-ton pickup with a two-ton load. No word from Becca, and I assumed none from her friends in Hot Springs. No word from Dennis and none from Falcon. I was surprised about him not calling until I remembered his comment about Raphael's family. "I bet he's taking care of them."

"What's that?"

Realizing I spoke my last thought aloud, I turned to our paralegal, Gretchen Love. "Sorry, Gretchen. My mind's wandering today."

"Me too," she said.

We took this as a reason to head for the break room. I haven't shared any details about the killings with the folks here. Most know of my dive out of the truck, but were unaware of the reasons behind it. Now I was wishing I could include them in our "inner circle." I felt like talking to someone.

I debated with myself but decided not to include Gretchen. We opted for light topics over coffee. Exhausting the clothing subject, we turned to men. Her love life wasn't a whole lot better than mine. When she finished, I covered Dennis—our on-again, off-again relationship and the fact we never "consummated" the arrangement.

"Me either," she said referring to the most recent male on her list. "I can't remember the last time I had sex."

I looked at the wall clock and Gretchen's gaze followed mine. We agreed it was time to return to our desks.

I managed to accomplish a little work. Midafternoon and still no phone calls. I dialed Falcon's cell again. No answer. By now his voice mailbox was full and not accepting any more messages. I fumed but decided it would get me nowhere. I wanted to talk with him about our latest postcard. I could only hope he would reactivate his phone and wade through the pile of messages.

Five o'clock came and I packed up my belongings. I felt a twinge of guilt as I reviewed the day's accomplishments in my mind. The temperature was moderate so I put the top down on my Mustang. I swung onto I-630 heading west, kicked it up to sixty and relaxed for the cruise home. Checking traffic in my mirrors, I noticed a white Cadillac Escalade two cars behind me—and felt it was not the first time I saw this car since getting on the interstate. I changed lanes, then pulled back into my original lane.

The SUV did the same. Looking around, I wondered why there was never a cop nearby when you need one. The easiest option that occurred to me was to accelerate and see if I could draw a cop's attention. The speedometer hovered around eighty-five and the SUV was hanging on my tail. I cut lanes again and he followed. I edged up to ninety and hung onto the wheel with all my might. A blowout at this speed could be downright hazardous to my health. Another hazard would soon be approaching—the traffic signal where I-630 ends and continues as Financial Centre Parkway. I didn't have the foggiest notion of my next move when I got there.

As I passed the interchange at Grant Street I saw one of LRPD's finest hauling ass with lights and siren moving along the westbound on-ramp. Glancing in my rear view, I yelled at the SUV, "Now, let's see if you've got any hair on your private parts." I stuck my arm up into the wind and gave him the universal gesture. I eased off the gas and edged onto the shoulder as the police car came up behind me. The SUV passed me and I saw the driver—he wore a clear plastic mask and the vehicle grew smaller as he continued down the road. In my excitement, I neglected to get a license plate number. I reminded myself it was no doubt stolen. Before he disappeared altogether, I could see movement—he was pulling the mask off.

I waited in my seat, both hands on the top of the steering wheel. When the officer approached, he glanced into the backseat and said, "Well, little lady. Just where's the fire?"

"Up there in that white SUV I believe was following me."

He glanced down the road, but it was too late for him to see anything. "License, registration and proof of insurance," he said.

I began my explanation as I produced the requested documents. The mention of Detective Sergeant Dennis Epstein and Lieutenant Oliver peaked his curiosity. He retreated to his squad car and I could see him busy on the radio. After a few minutes, he returned. "I don't know what this is all about, ma'am, but you got a couple of high ranks who vouch for you. Sergeant Epstein asks that you call him when you get home…and Lieutenant Oliver says I should escort you home to make sure the guy don't come back." He saluted and added, "Next time you want to attract attention, I suggest you dial nine-one-one."

I thanked him and waited until he was in his car before accelerating back into traffic. The policeman watched me pull into my parking garage and saluted once more before he drove away. I put the top up on my car and got out. The weakness in my legs surprised me. I took a minute to recover then made my way to my eighth-floor condo.

I was halfway through a tall glass of Beringer White Merlot when Effie arrived home from work. She joined me as I related the details of my trip home. We talked for a few minutes, then I made the rounds on the phone. Becca—no response from her code breakers. Falcon—voice mail still full. Dennis—answered on the third ring.

"Glad to hear your voice," he said. "Guess speeding's one way to get attention on the street."

"Worked for me." I took another sip of wine.

"Did you get a good look at the guy following you?"

"Yes and no. I saw him, but he wore the same mask as before, so I still don't know what he looks like."

"He seems to be getting bolder. Does Falcon still have someone trailing you?"

I thought about Raphael lying dead in the lobby and wondered if Falcon put another agent on the job. "Don't think so, and I haven't been able to reach Falcon."

"I'll arrange for a uniform to follow you to work in the morning. He'll identify himself using my name. Same thing for your drive home. It'll have to be a different officer because of shift changes."

I asked him if he thought our guy was going to come after me again. It was obvious there was no real answer for the question, but he warned me. His theory revolved around the idea the killer might want to capture and hold me as a witness to his next murder. I got a tingling chill up my spine hearing that one. He told me the department was not making any progress on the encrypted message from the postcard. When I asked him if lack of progress meant they were ignoring it, he bristled. I could hear it in his voice and defensive words like "we're doing our best."

I made a decision. It was time to start carrying my pistol-holster purse with my Glock nine-mil installed. I didn't tell Dennis. The last time I carried the gun we had a huge brouhaha. He didn't think I was capable of using it. I showed him…ended up killing two guys. Choking bile still rises in my throat whenever I think about that day in the Midtown Atrium Towers Building. Even though there was no choice, today I retch the same way I did then—both times.

I shared my idea with Effie and she agreed with me on both accounts—good idea to carry the weapon—bad idea to tell Dennis. We dragged out our copies of the latest postcard and stared.

```
pznenp       oziab7       bqlfdn

    6qc4li       7qp24p"
```

I looked up at Effie and said, "You got any idea how to go about solving this damn thing?"

"I've done a few cryptograms in the newspapers, but I bet this one is a lot more complicated than those."

I ought blank paper and a couple of pencils from the den. We both doodled l our wineglasses were empty. I said, "If no one gets to the bottom of this message, someone is going to die tomorrow night."

33

LAST NIGHT, I DREAMED OF A MAN IN A PLASTIC MASK killing people. Each time, he used a different weapon: rock, gun, ax. Then I was at the scene of the next murder. I couldn't see his weapon this time. I couldn't see the location. He was on his way to kill and I was following him. Or…was he already done?

Half asleep and staggering through the condo, I saw signs telling me Aaron returned during the night. Best of all was the aroma of coffee coming from the kitchen. Aaron sat with his feet on a chair, a paper propped in front of him, and a cup of steaming coffee in his hand. His head came up as I entered and he said, "What's new?"

"Man, have I got news." I told him about Raphael's death in the lobby and the latest postcard. I raced to the dining room where we left copies of the card and back to the kitchen. "We figured out the message. Refers to *The Big Sleep* by Raymond Chandler. We've got no idea what the coded part means. Do you know how to solve encrypted messages?" I was out of breath, so I shut up.

Aaron studied the papers, sipped his coffee and made unintelligible grunting sounds. "Elementary, my dear Watson. I don't have the foggiest," he said.

"If our crackpot holds to his schedule, I figure we've got about twelve hours before he kills again. The police don't seem interested in helping, but Becca has some high schoolkids working on the code." I explained her connection to the advanced school in Hot Springs and covered my discussion with Dennis. "You know anyone who could help?" He shook his head.

I considered calling in sick at work, discarded the idea and returned to my room. Half hour later I was on my way out the door. Aaron handed me a bagel saying I needed something on my stomach. He said, "I'll be home all day. Call me if I can help."

I thanked him and asked if he would update Effie. I grabbed a copy of the latest card and was out the door at seven forty-five. I pulled out of my parking garage and saw the same police officer from yesterday. He put two fingers to the bill of his cap in a salute and he kept an eye on me until I entered my office building. I'll have to thank Dennis for the concern again today.

My law research was interesting and I was surprised to see half the morning slipped away before I started clock-watching. Time to take a break and make a few phone calls. I confirmed Becca was at work at TrueTemp. She said there was no word from the whiz kids yet. During a call to Dennis, we each promised to contact one another if anything new arose. Thinking it was a waste of time, I punched in Falcon's number. Two rings, a click, another ring and he answered. "What's up, Casey?"

"How's Raphael's family?" I said. He told me he was still with them. They were devastated and he said there would be a memorial service on Friday. I asked him how they were financially.

He said, "I've been damn fortunate in my business. I set up four trusts—one for Rosa, his wife, and one for each of his children. He has a ten-year-old daughter and twin boys around six."

He paused, and from the tone of his voice I wondered if a tear was forming in his eye. Did he ever in his life cry or shed a tear? "That seems more than generous," I said.

"He lost his life doing what I asked him to do."

"You asked him? Wasn't he working for you?"

"Nothing formal. I called and he came. I don't ever remember him turning me down. I owe him for the loyalty. If money is the only way I can repay that debt, so be it."

Sounded like we were at the end of this topic. I told him about the coded message.

"Damn. I should have checked with you sooner. I know people with computer access who should be able to help. It may take a few hours to call in some chits and get them rolling. Since he's giving us warning, our guy may hit earlier than usual…say around eight tonight. That only gives us a little over nine hours to get an answer and be in place."

He was quiet and I decided not to interrupt what was no doubt a thought process. He came back. "Is the coded message in a form you can read it to me?" I told him it was. "Read it. Tell me exactly how it's laid out on the page—rows, spaces, whatever—don't leave anything out."

I did as he asked then said, "When will you get back to me?" I waited for a moment before I realized he was no longer on the other end of the phone.

34

ROMEO GLANCED OVER HIS SHOULDER…AGAIN. IT was part of his routine since Tuesday night and it was now midday Thursday. He found himself unnerved at having to kill the Mexican last Tuesday. Romeo did not like unscheduled events. He took solace in the fact his reactions, even though surprised, were swift and decisive. There was nothing suspicious behind him and for the first time in two days he allowed himself to smile.

He scouted this place last night and was back now to confirm everything in the light of day. Strolling by the construction site north of the eleven-thousand block of Chenal Parkway, he wondered how business would be at this new Chinese restaurant. A lot of people will not want to eat at a murder scene, he thought.

Slipping the lock on the chain link gate was simple. Duping the victim was easy as well. The man he met through a business contact was on the fringe of the criminal world. Connections were remote; the chances of tracing the man back to Romeo would be difficult if not impossible. The fact Romeo did not want a cut of the theft surprised him. Romeo countered saying he might ask for a favor at a later date. The prospect of copper plumbing and easy access were irresistible.

Romeo walked, in his mind, through each step he would take tonight. Pick up the man in a stolen car. Park nearby. Walk to the site and open the gate. Escort the victim by showing him where the kitchen and bathrooms—the most lucrative areas— were located. In the back of the building's interior, in the darkest recesses, Romeo's silenced pistol would finish the job. For this one, he opted for a revolver. It would be noisier than the automatic, but with it, there would be no ejected shell casings to search for in the dark.

Romeo felt the sensation between his legs even though he was going through the steps only in his mind. He knew the feeling would be more intense tonight. And…if those idiots who were out to stop him managed to break his code…the thought of the chase heightened his anticipation.

He returned to his car and his mind worked all the harder. Maybe Casey will be the one to solve the instructions. It would be so wonderful if she were here to share the evening with me. He pictured her standing beside him, holding his arm, as he shot his latest present to her. He leaned back in the seat as the wave of the orgasm swept over him. "Casey," he said, "you must yield soon. I do not know how long I can keep this up."

35

LATE AFTERNOON AND GATHERING CLOUDS WERE visible from the office windows. It would be dark earlier tonight than the date would indicate. I made the rounds on the phone and the news was disappointing. No one offered encouragement. While talking to Becca, we arranged to meet for dinner near my home.

Mickey's hands crawled toward five o'clock. I packed my work away and left the building for my Mustang. I stopped near the police car as I pulled out, and he mentioned Dennis' name to confirm his bona fides.

I stopped long enough to tell the officer I was going to a restaurant rather than home. "I'll be meeting a friend there and should be safe." He was the same officer who followed me home yesterday. He gave me a two-finger salute and swung his car around behind me when I accelerated down the street.

I slid my car into a slot in the restaurant lot. Becca was already parked and started toward me. I got out, gave the cop an "okay" sign and he pulled away. I felt safe, figuring our bad guy would be too busy tonight to be thinking of me.

We spent over an hour eating and another forty-five minutes discussing what might happen tonight. I was already calculating a generous tip for our waiter. After all, we were burning up his income producing time. We reached the foyer on our way out when Becca's cell phone rang.

"This may be it," she said. From then on, her side of the conversation was sparse and I wasn't able to glean anything. Then she tucked the phone between ear and shoulder and made wild gestures like someone writing a note. It dawned on me she needed writing materials. Fumbling in my purse, I dragged out a pen and a small pad of sticky notes.

Becca scratched away while juggling to keep the phone up to her ear. I couldn't see what she was writing and an occasional grunt did nothing to enhance my understanding. The look on her face seemed to mirror the frustration I was feeling.

She was on her fourth sticky note when she said, "Enough already with the details. You can email them to me later. For now, cut to the chase—what does the damn translated message say?"

A couple more grunts, an "ah-ha" and she punched the END button on her cell. "They wanted to give me the blow-by-blow details on how they solved the code."

"Well?"

"It says, and I quote, 'about 11000 chenal parkway come watch.' "

"I'm not sure that helps," I said. "How much does that narrow things down?"

Becca said, "I think I saw a sign on the way over here. It advertised a new Chinese restaurant in the area. Could that be a tie-in to the reference in the note?"

I pulled out my phone and dialed Dennis. We discussed the solution to the coded message and he said he was on his way. He also told me to sit tight and not get involved.

"That's not likely to happen," I said. "Besides, we're a whole heck of a lot closer than you are." Becca pointed to herself and made a steering wheel motion. "Keep an eye out for Becca's car." I described the green Firebird and rang off before he could protest further.

We jogged to her car. She put a hand on the top of the windshield and the other on the driver's closed door, then vaulted in behind the wheel. "Imagine me doing that six months ago," she shouted with a grin. I eyeballed the opening the missing half of the T-top gave me on the passenger's side. I opted for the door handle.

In a single fluid motion, Becca wheeled the car out of the parking place, reversed course and headed for the street. The lot was large and not laid out well so arrows were painted to keep the lanes flowing. Becca paid no attention to the attempts to direct traffic and plowed forward.

I was busy hauling out my cell again. Falcon and Aaron, in that order, were my next calls. Aaron said he could be in the area in about twenty minutes. It would take Falcon much longer since he was up near the air force base, fifteen to twenty miles northeast of the city.

"You carrying that purse you told me about?" Falcon said.

I said, "Yes,"

Before he rang off, he added, "Be careful. If you have to use the damn thing, make each one count."

Becca was revving the engine and running through the gears like a pro. It was a large parking lot with several hard turns before reaching the street. Even corners didn't slow her down. "Where did you learn to drive like that?" I said.

"When I trimmed the last twenty-five pounds off, I treated myself to a driving course. Ever hear of the Bondurant Driving School in Phoenix?" When I said nothing, she continued in a voice loud enough to be heard over the engine roar and the squeal of tires. "It's damned expensive, but worth every penny. I can do anything with this car—even make it sit up on its rear wheels and beg." She looked at me and must have seen some horror on my face. "Relax, Casey. I'm only kidding about the begging."

We bounced over the lot entrance and hit the street above the legal speed limit. Becca's hands and feet were of blur of action. She banged the transmission into the next gear and buried her foot into the floorboard. I saw a corner coming but assumed she would take a different route. When she downshifted and cut the wheel, I screamed, "Way too fast." Guess it wasn't since we completed the ninety-degree left-hander and accelerated back up to her previous speed, which a glance at the speedometer told me was over sixty.

"I think we need a right here," Becca said straining her lungs.

I stuck my hand out toward her and signaled "yes." At the same time, I dug my feet into the firewall and braced for another mind-bending turn. Centrifugal forces hit me and when I opened my eyes again, we were accelerating straight ahead. My cell phone rang. Caller ID told me it was Dennis. I answered and heard, "Casey, don't you go near the crime scene. Where are you?"

I gave him an approximate location, and said we were about three minutes from the area. "We still have to find the exact spot. Stop worrying."

Becca locked up all four wheels and slid over to the curb. "This is the eleven-thousand block on Chenal, where the hell do we go from here? Where did I see that dang construction site?" she said.

For the first time since we left the parking lot, I noticed a fine mist was falling. "For damn sure it's not here. Must be north or south of this street. Make a choice."

She sat for a few seconds, looked both directions and jerked the car into first gear. Becca took the next street to the north and we cruised the parallel street. Then we saw it—a building under construction—and the sign in front said: Loo Fong Chinese Restaurant, Opening Soon. Becca eased the Firebird to the curb, killed the headlights and we sat there listening and peering into the darkness. Even in idle, the twin exhausts on the Firebird rumbled.

Becca swung her arm toward me and slammed me on the chest then pointed at the building under construction. Staring into the gloom, I saw a pinpoint of light dancing over the ground near what would be the front door. A figure moved at a slow pace as if picking its way through a minefield. The man, if it was a man, stopped, frozen in place. The point of light went dark and the figure scurried toward a corner of the building and disappeared moving toward the rear of the lot.

"He's trying to get away," I said. "I bet he's got a car parked on the street back there." Becca shifted into gear, flicked on the headlights and we were gunning away from the curb. She found a street, made a hard left and then another left and we were nearing the rear of the construction site. There were cars parked on both sides of the street and she slowed so we could get a better look at each one. We were a half-block past the rear of the Chinese restaurant when a car behind us screeched out of a parking place headed the opposite direction. The sound alerted us because it didn't have any lights on. Becca stopped, sped up hard in reverse and yelled, "Watch this."

She had an arm over the back of her seat so she could hold a straight course down the lanes between the parked cars. Becca shifted her body forward, cut the steering wheel and hit the brakes while she shifted into a forward gear. The car snapped around one hundred and eighty degrees as she completed a J-turn. We were headed the opposite direction in hot pursuit of the killer's vehicle. Our only visual clue was a pair of dim taillights disappearing into the night.

"He turned," Becca said. "Did you see which way he went?"

"Right, I think."

"Here's hoping you're right." Becca hit the brakes, then accelerated through the turn.

What appeared to be the same taillights were ahead of us and much closer. "If that's him," I said, "I bet he's moving slow so he doesn't draw attention."

As soon as the Firebird's headlamps lit up the fleeing car, it began to accelerate.

"That's him for damn sure," Becca said, her foot stomping the gas pedal down even harder.

The pursuit continued through residential streets. The guy was good, but lacked Becca's driving skills. We gained on him at every turn. I realized Dennis was still en route to the Chenal address. He answered as soon as his cell rang. I told him where we were—as best I could. I didn't know the neighborhood and all the course changes made it even more difficult.

"Hang on a sec," Dennis said.

I could hear his voice in the distance talking to someone. It dawned on me he put his cell down and was speaking on the police radio.

Our target made a hard right and disappeared around the corner. Not to worry, I thought, as soon as Becca makes the turn he'll be in sight again.

Surprise. Around the corner we went and the street was empty. Becca eased off the gas while we did our best to pick him out. The roadway was well lit from streetlights and business signs. I said, "No way he got far enough ahead to disappear like this." Our heads were swiveling around. "There's only one answer.—he's still here." I finished the words as we neared several cars parked on the right.

When we came abreast of the second of the parked cars, Becca jerked the gear lever and shouted: GUN.

36

WHEN BECCA SHOUTED, I DUCKED AND HEARD THREE explosions. She was on the gas pedal—hard.

I still had my phone to my ear and Dennis was yelling, "What the hell is going on?"

Becca braked to a stop a block away. We craned our necks and watched our quarry complete a U-turn, then a right turn and disappear.

I brought Dennis up to speed between his curses and several I-told-you-not-to's. I said we would meet him at the Chinese restaurant and ended the call. I looked at Becca. She was shaking and I couldn't decide if it was fear or rage.

"That son-of-a-bitch shot at my car," Becca said. She left the car idling, set the hand brake and got out. Walking around the car, she caressed it with loving care. She came around the rear and moved up the passenger side. Becca stopped and shouted, "Son-of-a-bitch." She poked a finger into a hole in the side about twelve inches behind the passenger seat. "Son-of-a-bitch." She stuck her head in my window and said, "You okay?"

I extended my arm so she would not have to tear her eyes away from the task at hand and gave her a thumbs-up. She checked the right front and returned to the trunk area. The mist was turning into a fine rain and I realized I was getting wet. At the speeds we'd traveled, the windshield had hurled the damp mess up and over the open T-top. Now, sitting still, the rain penetrated the interior.

From an open trunk, Becca produced the half-cover for my seat and installed it. She repeated the process for the opening above her seat, climbed in and said, "There's a hole in the side of my car. Son…of…a…bitch."

By the time we retraced our route to the restaurant, Dennis and a squad car were parked in front. Headlights and spotlights were trained on the construction site. Becca pulled up next to the police car and added another pair of high beams to the illumination.

Dennis stopped long enough to tell us to stay put. He sent one of the officers around the building while he and the other policeman went in the front. It didn't take five minutes for the three of them to complete their journey. One officer retrieved a large roll of yellow tape from his car and began stringing it in front of the building.

"That tells me we've got a crime scene," I said to Becca.

Dennis approached our car. "Guy dead in the kitchen area. Three gunshot wounds to the chest. Tight pattern. My guess is, all three hit the heart."

"Another matching detail," Becca said.

Dennis looked confused.

Becca said, "The dead guy in *The Big Sleep* got a triple tap to the chest. This murder matches the latest postcard." She got out of her door, walked around the right side and pointed. "Son-of-a-bitch shot a hole in my car."

Dennis looked at me and said, "You didn't tell me about any shooting. Anyone hit?"

"There were at least three shots fired. One hit us and the other two…got no idea."

By this time, two other police cars arrived on the scene. Dennis told the pair in one car to follow us back to the scene of the shooting. We did that and pointed out where the bad guy's car was parked when he fired. The policemen took over the area, called for backup and began outlining the area with yellow tape. Deciding there was nothing more we could accomplish here, Becca and I got ready to leave for my house but decided to return to the restaurant.

We milled around the restaurant area for a few minutes and before we could get back into the car, Aaron arrived. I told him he missed all the action, but we could discuss it at home. Becca drove at a more sedate rate than earlier, and I was able to contact Falcon. He said he would see us at my place.

Aaron and Falcon joined us in the parking garage. Becca opened her trunk and said, "Hang on, let me get a bag outta here. I figured it might be a long night so I packed a change of clothes." She looked at me. "Okay if I spend the night?"

I put an arm around her and we headed toward the elevator. When we entered the lobby, my neighbor, Kenley, turned from the mailboxes and greeted us. "Good evening, Casey. And…a good evening to all of you too."

Since he didn't know Falcon and Becca, I completed the introductions. He nodded to each of them. Turning to Aaron, he said, "How good it is to see you as well, young man." He smiled a large, large smile.

It was difficult to tell, but I'm sure Aaron blushed.

Kenley asked the reason we were all out at this hour and added, "Does it have something to do with the gentleman who was killed here on Tuesday?"

I explained we couldn't go into detail, but the basic answer was yes. The five of us rode up to the eighth floor where I said goodnight to Kenley. The rest of us entered my home.

Effie joined us. Becca and I told our story of the chase, the shots and the return to the murder scene. Effie asked if we saw the victim. "Dennis didn't want us inside the building. Besides, this one was no doubt like the others. Someone picked at random—in the wrong place at the wrong time."

Falcon said, "What makes you think that, Casey?"

"Well, so far there doesn't seem to be anything in common about the victims. Other than the same guy, our nutcase, did them all."

"Not quite true," he said. "The one commonality is you, Casey."

Those words sent cold shivers up and down my spine.

Effie popped up and announced, "I think it's time for some wine. Anyone have a preference?" When no one responded, she said, "I'll bring red and white and you can decide later."

Aaron went to the kitchen to lend a hand. I looked at Becca who appeared to be unaffected by the whole evening. I leaned toward her and said, "How the hell can you look so calm after what we went through?"

"Calm exterior, inside I'm churning. It's a coping mechanism I suppose. I'm mad as hell the twerp shot a hole in my car."

"How far were you from the other car when he fired?" Falcon said.

We both sat there staring into space. I figured we were both trying to picture the scene—at least that's what I was doing. We began to speak at the same time and I waved for Becca to start.

"I'm guessing, but I'd say eight to ten feet."

Falcon said, "Where was your car in relation to the other one when he fired the first shot?"

I jumped in. "We were right next to him."

Falcon asked his next question. "Becca, were you accelerating by then?"

"Yes, I think so."

After a minute of reflection, Falcon continued, "Two possibilities. One, he's a bad shot, which I doubt. Two, he saw you, Casey and didn't want to hit you. So, he aimed behind you. I wonder if the police found where the other two rounds hit."

Picking up my cell phone, I said, "Maybe Dennis can give us an update on that."

Effie returned with the wine and I turned my back so I could concentrate on my call. I reached Dennis on the third try. He told me the crime scene folks didn't find any trace of the other two shots. Most of the storefronts on the opposite side of the street were glass and none had a bullet hole. The investigators were extending the search to the upper floor exteriors of those buildings. "So, far, nada," he said. "I've got to go now. Call me later, okay?"

I told him I would and turned around to find a huge glass of white wine in front of me. Nodding a salute to Effie, I took a large swig. "Dennis says this crime scene is like all the rest. No evidence, no nothing. They didn't find bullet holes in the buildings across the street from where we were shot at."

"I think your guy missed you on purpose," Falcon said. "He had you cold, Casey. From the distance you described, I don't see how he could have missed—so it must have been on purpose."

Becca sat up. "Do you think he could have hit us both if he wanted to?"

"Yes." Falcon nodded. "He's killed two people with a gun. No reason to think he isn't good with one."

"Sorry I didn't get there earlier," Aaron said. "Maybe I could have helped in the chase."

Falcon and I started to speak at the same time. He waved, inviting me to go first.

"I'm not sure you could keep up with Becca here. She took a driving course in Arizona, and she wheels her Firebird like a professional." Becca smiled and lowered her eyes, doing her best to look demur.

Falcon put on an expression of approval and nodded his head. "Bondurant?" he said.

Becca perked up and launched into a description of the high-speed, high-performance driving skills the company teaches.

"I've always wanted to do that," Effie said.

More than one incredulous look was displayed around the table. Becca jumped in. "Then you should do it. Let me know if you decide to go for it—I'll come along. I'd love to take the course again."

"From what I saw tonight," I said. "You don't need a refresher."

When the laughter subsided, Falcon spoke. It was a more serious tone as he said, "Raphael's memorial service is tomorrow

morning at ten-thirty." He named the church and provided directions. "I think he would appreciate your being there."

Over another glass of wine, we talked about Raphael. I started
to tell about Falcon's generous contribution to the family but
didn't get more that three words out. He caught my attention
and shook his head, indicating I should change the subject,
which I did. The others at the table looked perplexed but didn't
press the issue.

We all agreed to attend Raphael's service and coordinated
our transportation.

My phone rang and I left the table to answer it.

A voice said, "Hi, Casey. It is me."

I didn't recognize the caller. "So, who the hell is me?"

"Romeo…your admirer."

"Okay, who the hell is Romeo?"

"My dear, Casey. Tsk, tsk, such language. I am certain you
remember going for a ride with me on the interstate. It is just
that you have not been introduced to me by name."

37

IF MY TEETH WERE FALSE, THEY WOULD HAVE POPPED out of my mouth. With wild arm waves, I got the attention of those still sitting at the table. When they were looking at me, I jabbed an index finger at the phone and mouthed: It's him. It's him.

Falcon dashed to his small briefcase then approached me. By the time he arrived, he was holding two items in his hand. He licked the suction cup and applied it to the back of my handset then pressed the record button. He nodded to me.

"Why did you call me?" I said.

Romeo said, "I thought it was time we talked, Casey. I hope you are recovered from your ordeal of jumping from my vehicle."

I did my best to put a face with the voice. No luck. Sounds like he's muffling the sound, I thought. The level as well as the tone changed with an irregular rhythm. But something was familiar. "I'm okay, no thanks to you."

"I am sorry you feel that way, Casey. Any injuries you sustained are the result of your own actions. How are you feeling? I notice you are no longer wearing the sling for your arm."

Doing my best not to sound surprised he's been close enough to see me, I said, "I'm doing okay."

Romeo said, "Congratulations on solving my latest message. You are indeed a resourceful lady."

Falcon pulled out his cell phone and dialed. He put his hands up in front of him and gave me a signal—one a TV floor manager might use to tell the on-air person to drag out the presentation.

I thanked Romeo for his compliment, and said, "You're a pretty good driver."

"Yes, I am. The black lady driving the car you were in is an excellent driver as well. Tell me, did you solve the cryptogram yourself?"

I told him we received help, but danced around his question looking for a more detailed answer.

"Have you also solved the other part of the postcard messages?" he said. "And...the tie-ins to the deaths?"

"The last one refers to the murder mystery *The Big Sleep*."

"Not bad," he said. "I bet you have not solved them all."

Thinking about Falcon's "stretch" signal, I hemmed and hawed before I began listing the cards in sequence. *The Maltese Falcon*, by Dashiell Hammett...Edgar Allan Poe's *The Black Cat*...*The Five Orange Pips* by Sir Arthur Conan Doyle" The following pause was so long I was afraid Romeo was no longer on the phone. "Are you still there?"

"Yes," he said, "I was thinking you are not only resourceful, but also extremely intelligent and well read. Did you solve them on your own?"

Remembering his earlier attempt to get more details, I decided to focus the attention on me. "I did it by my lonesome."

"Casey, I believe I must impugn your veracity. I doubt that any person—beyond me, that is—would be capable of deciphering my cryptic messages. I rather suspect Aaron Kincaid, Effie Tremayne, Rebecca Rider and that Falcon person may have assisted you. Tell those people for me, anyone attempting to thwart my plans will be dealt with in the most severe terms... think terminate with extreme prejudice."

There was another long pause and I experienced the same fear as before.

At last he said, "I will be seeing you soon, Casey."

Again, another pause and this time when I asked if he was still on the line, there was no answer. I shook my head at Falcon and he retrieved his recorder. "Who's on the phone with you?" I said.

Falcon said, "It's Sergeant Epstein." Then he held up a hand, palm out in front of me. "Okay, Sergeant. Sorry we couldn't keep him on the phone longer…of course, I'll get you a copy of the recording."

When we gathered at the table again, Falcon covered his conversation with Dennis. "The police were able to trace the call—to some extent. It was an untraceable throw-away cell. The call was made from somewhere near the River Market—too much of a crowd they didn't get near anyone on a cell phone."

He played the recording for everyone. When the message neared its end, all those mentioned on the tape, save Falcon, seemed shaken. It dawned on me, perhaps I should feel threatened as well—figured I was since my hands were shaking. I also wondered what Romeo meant when he said he'd see me soon.

Falcon replayed the last part of the message. When the words ended, he said, "Seems obvious, he has access to high-tech equipment. I doubt we'll be able to clear the distortion and get anywhere close to his real voice."

Our discussions lasted past midnight without any definitive answers. Falcon played the full message on his recorder to Dennis and again promised to send a copy to the police, or Dennis could pick it up. They decided on the latter. The last order of business was to confirm our plans for the morning. Everyone would be attending the memorial service for Raphael.

38

I TUNED TO THE EARLY MORNING SHOW ON TV AND they verified my guess about today—overcast, light drizzle all day. I wondered if it was a fit day for a memorial service. Whether it was or not, it's Friday and in a few hours, they will be saying kind things about a man I knew because Falcon asked him to watch over me. I knew I would have a hard time keeping it together. Even thinking about it now made my eyes misty.

Becca and I joined my roomies in the kitchen. Effie was in the midst of another one of her culinary masterpieces. Perhaps I exaggerate—for me it would have been a masterpiece, for her it was a simple meal—huevos rancheros. Aaron asked for seconds. Becca and I stared at him like he was out of his mind. The first helping Effie was putting on our plates seemed enough to feed a small army.

"What?" Aaron said in response to our scowls. "I'm a growing boy."

We discussed the events of last evening. Whew, what a night—murder, car chase, shot at and the piece de resistance, a phone call from our nutcase who calls himself Romeo.

While we were still at breakfast, Dennis arrived with an audio specialist. They made dupes of the recorded call. Since Falcon was using a digital recorder, the audio guy transferred the call to his own machine. I asked him for a copy on a cassette. He wasn't inclined to fulfill my request until Dennis interceded. Then Dennis left with his audio specialist saying he would meet us at the church.

I held up the audio cassette and said to those around the breakfast table, "Anyone want to hear the guy again?"

Everyone nodded and I hurried to the computer room to get a portable player. I popped the plastic case into the machine and hit the PLAY button. The recording seemed short. When the call ended, I hit the rewind and played it again. Keeping an eye on my watch, I talked to him for only three minutes or so. On the phone last night, it seemed like the call took an eternity.

Effie and Aaron excused themselves saying they needed to get ready for the service. I said, "Becca, you can take your shower first. I'll be along in a minute." Alone, I listened to the phone call one more time. I've heard his voice—on the tape and in person when I was sitting not two feet away from him during the kidnapping. In my mind, I went over the "bad guy" list I put together. With all that, I was no closer to identifying who he could be. I suppose this rules out Aaron and Falcon, I told myself.

I closed my eyes and leaned back. An old familiar tingling was moving up and down my spine. What does he really want to do? What does he want with me? Scenario after scenario played out in my mind. In the final one I pictured myself facing him with a gun in my hand. I've killed two human beings and was violently ill both times. I even tossed the old cookies a third time and didn't shoot anyone then. If it came to a matter of him or me, could I pull the trigger again?

I came back to the real world when Becca called my name. I headed for my room planning on a long shower.

The hot water on my back was soothing and I closed my eyes again. I couldn't get the images of dead men out of my head. "I don't think I can do it again." I opened my eyes, wiped condensation from the glass door and looked to be sure no one heard me.

I rode into town with Becca so she could drop me at the restaurant where we ate last night. I still needed to pick up my car and get to work after the memorial service. I called my office and the boss at the law firm told me to take my time getting to work. Effie rode with Aaron and Dennis would meet us at the cathedral.

We arrived at the church near downtown Little Rock about the same time. Like most, there were towers, spires and a wealth of stained glass. There were twenty minutes to spare so we chatted outside and did some people watching. Effie spotted our neighbor Kenley Longstreet and I went to greet him. He said he saw the notice in the newspaper and decided to attend. Kenley excused himself and entered the church.

When I returned to my group Aaron pointed out my ex, Jarvis, in the crowd. Who else is going to show up out of the blue? I made my way to where he was standing looking like a lost—lost something. "What are you doing here?"

"Oh. I came to be here for you, Casey." He stared at me with a blank face. "I know this guy meant something to you."

"How do you know that?"

"You must have mentioned his name one time when we were talking. I saw the name in the newspaper…"

Shaking my head, I left him standing there and made my way back to Becca and the others. I don't remember telling Jarvis about Raphael, but I suppose I could have.

Aaron checked his watch, moved toward the door and said, "Shall we?" The five of us started inside. I caught sight of someone in my peripheral vision. The guy seemed familiar. We were already inside the church when I turned around. I felt like a salmon headed upstream at mating season. I excused myself and pushed back outside. Looking to the right where I saw the man before, he was no longer in sight.

"Damn," I whispered under my breath. "Who the devil was that?"

A lady going the opposite direction and wearing a huge black hat with an even larger feather looked at me and sidestepped. From the look on her face she no doubt figured me for a raving heretic talking to the devil. I turned and rejoined the throng pouring inside.

I found my friends, who were saving me a seat. "Where did you go?" Effie said.

When I finished explaining my absence, Dennis leaned over. "Could it have been our guy?"

I told him it was possible and he stood up. "I don't think there's a chance of finding him out there," I said.

He pushed toward me and asked what the man was wearing. "Nondescript," I said. "Tan topcoat, I think."

Edging out of our row, Dennis hurried up the aisle toward the main entrance. He put his cell phone to his ear and that's the last we saw of him.

Falcon was seated in the front row with Raphael's family. Next to him was an attractive Hispanic woman who looked too young to be a widow—but she was. I could see the twin boys and the daughter Falcon told me about. Both boys fidgeted in their seats and tugged at the collars of the white shirts they wore. They looked far too young to grasp the finality of this memorial to their father. The girl—how old did Falcon say she was? Ten, I think—was prim, head down, dabbing at her eyes with a tissue. She knows he's gone forever, I thought.

The scent of lighted candles and incense brought back memories of times long ago when I attended church more often than today. As usual, at times like these, I was not able to hold the tears back. I pulled out the first handkerchief—there was a spare in my purse because I figured this for a two-hankie event. I hoped the words the priest spoke were comforting for the widow and children. I found I was still unable to accept words like "working in mysterious ways" as a comfort. Falcon gave the eulogy and spoke from the heart. I was forced to drag out my spare handkerchief. Twice there was a catch in his voice as he used Raphael's name. I got the impression he delivered more than his share of speeches such as this. And that when he did, a little bit of him died as well—maybe a large bit. I wondered if he would be willing to share with someone—me.

The spectators waited for Raphael's family to leave and the ushers directed us to file out, row by row. Outside, I looked for Jarvis and Kenley. They were nowhere in sight, nor was the semi-familiar figure in the brown coat. I assumed Dennis was in hot pursuit of our phantom mourner.

The memorial service filled the first part of the day. I put in a short half-day at work. Word about my involvement in the killing spree was spreading. I couldn't figure how it got to my office, but they all had ties to the legal, police and PI community. Three people did their best to question me. I dodged the issues and avoided any substantial answers.

I got my usual police escort from the office to my home. I checked in with Dennis on arrival and promised him I'd call if I planned to go anywhere over the weekend.

* * *

I was looking forward to a quiet day with the Sunday papers. I grabbed a cup of coffee and joined Aaron at the kitchen table. He slid a section toward me and said, "Take a look at the front page, below the fold."

I did as he suggested and froze. The article caption read: Post Card Killer on the Loose. I raced through the first page coverage and turned to page 12A for the continuation. The gist of the story was based on an anonymous source who was "close to the investigation and close to the person receiving the postcards." The details were sparse, but accurate enough to make me believe the "source" knew more than the average citizen. I wasn't identified except as a female living on the west side of Little Rock and working in the legal profession. Too damn close for my taste.

"How the hell does someone know this much about Romeo?" I said. "It's obvious he…or she doesn't know everything, but…"

Aaron shook his head and started to speak. He was interrupted by the phone, which he answered. After the pleasantries, he said, "Dennis," when he passed the handset to me.

Dennis said, "Have you seen this morning's newspaper?" When I said yes, he started in on me. "Who leaked it to the papers? Which one of your cohorts did it?"

"Wait just a damn minute," I said, hoping the disgust in my voice carried over to him. "What makes you think it was me or anyone I know? I resent your attitude and if you don't apologize, I'll hang up on you."

I was greeted with stuttering, "er's" and "ah's." "Well spit it out," I said.

"I'm sorry. My boss is all over me and I can't think of anyone who would do this—at least no one outside your group. What about Falcon?"

"When he calls, which I expect will be soon, I'll tell him you want me to ask."

"I don't suppose he has a motive…Casey, if you have any ideas, please let me know."

Effie was puttering around the kitchen by now. We showed her the paper and as soon as she finished the article, our conversation turned to the leaker's identity. We ran down a list of possibles, but we found ourselves shaking our heads at each name. When the phone rang again, I said, "Bet it's Falcon."

I was right. He and I went through the same conversation I had with Dennis. He couldn't come up with any creditable answers either. He indicated he would work on the source of the leak and get back to me later today or tomorrow.

Throughout the day, I kept coming back to the newspaper story. The waters didn't clear with further readings. I spent a fitful night and each time I woke, the same questions kept me awake. Who? What? What's next?

* * *

I found a Sunday front section on my desk when I arrived at work on Monday morning. No one owned up to putting it there and I didn't ask. I received a few arched eyebrows, but not a word was said. At nine-thirty Mr. Thomasen, the senior partner, summoned me to his office. I knocked, was invited in and entered.

"Close the door, Ms. Fremont."

We weren't on familiar terms, but the "Ms." caught me off guard. On several occasions in the past, he used my first name.

"I'm concerned for you," he said. He began rearranging items on his desktop. Seeming to be satisfied with the position of his pens and notepads, he looked up. "Casey, I know you are under pressure. I do not know all the details; however, it must be a strain." He decided the notepad was not in the correct spot and moved it to the opposite side of the desk. "Even knowing as little about you as I do, it is not difficult to figure out yesterday's news story was talking about you. I not only have to look out for you, but also look out for the reputation of this firm." It was time for the pens to be shifted around. "Do I have to worry you will become a detriment to us?"

39

I STARED AT MR. THOMASEN FOR A MINUTE AND DID my best to regain some composure. I said, "I don't know why everyone would assume I'm the subject of the article. Sure, the people around here—folks close to this office and me—might put two and two together. I don't think others will make such assumptions."

Worried I might be coming on too strong, I assured Mr. Thomasen I was fine and couldn't imagine causing any problems for his law firm. I wished I felt as good about the situation as my words conveyed. He closed our session with, "Let us know if we can do anything to help, Casey."

Arriving at home, I discovered another postcard in my mailbox. A duplicate of the others, but…this one was blank. I called Dennis and he stopped by later to take custody of the postcard.

By Wednesday I wondered if Romeo would kill someone this week. Thursday was his day. On Friday evening, our group gathered at my condo. Besides my roomies, Falcon, Dennis and Becca joined us. Dennis reported that there were no murders anywhere in Little Rock, or for that matter in the whole of Pulaski County.

Falcon stood. "Dennis, do you think our guy has stopped?"

"No. Serial killers don't just stop. They may take a breather, but our experience says he will strike again."

"In that case, what do we do now?" Effie said.

"We keep our guard up," Falcon said. He made a silent trip around the table as though he was pondering the situation. He had a knack of riveting attention on himself. By the time he took his seat again everyone's gaze was fixed on him. Then looking at Dennis, he added, "Can we count on the police to maintain their presence and protect Casey?"

"As far as I know, yes."

The discussion returned to the blank postcard left in my mailbox last Monday. Ideas were tossed out on the table. Falcon, said, "He's quit giving advance clues and will make the process harder. What else?"

"He is done—no more killings, but I doubt it," Effie said.

It was my turn. "Realizing there is no chance of impressing me, he is giving up."

Aaron said, "He's gone into hiding until the pressure on him relaxes."

None of these ideas took center stage, but all agreed Romeo would strike again.

With no consensus on his motives, we turned to the subject of his identity. Dennis recounted his attempt to find the stranger at Raphael's memorial service. "I didn't get close to anyone in a tan overcoat. Casey, has anything else come to your mind? Anything which would help tell us who he is?"

I admitted I couldn't even hazard a guess. "I've been within a couple of feet of this guy, this Romeo, and there is nothing that stands out in my mind to identify him." Feeling helpless, I changed the subject again. "Have you gotten a lead on who leaked the story to the newspaper?" I said to Dennis.

Dennis shook his head, and once again, no one at the table came up with a good guess.

Becca said, "It has to be someone close to one of us. How else could the leaker know about the postcards and Casey?"

"Everyone should think about people we've talked to—people who might have gathered the information," Aaron said.

Effie held up a hand. "What if it's someone who is making good guesses and filling in the blanks with conjecture?" Several of us gave her a give-us-more signal. "Well, who knows about the postcards?" We listed everyone we could think of: the six of us, the police, Romeo of course—but would he call the papers? We didn't think anyone on this list would be the culprit. Effie continued, "There's one person who knows about the postcards we haven't mentioned." Head shakes and frowns all around the table followed. "What about Mr. Kenley Longstreet?"

Effie said, "Remember, Mr. Longstreet brought us the post-card, which was inserted in his mailbox by mistake. And…he was around when Raphael's body was found here in the lobby. With direct information like that, it wouldn't take too much research to find more and tie it all together."

I wracked my brain trying to think if I told Kenley more about the case. I came up with a blank and asked the rest if they could remember telling him any of the details.

Falcon leaned in and said, "I think Effie's right. A little snoop-ing here and there, and he could have tied reported crimes to the postcard he saw. The rest could be good guesses." He stood and poured himself another glass of wine.

We exhausted a variety of guesses on the paper's story and got no closer to identifying Romeo. Our guests drifted out and before he left, Falcon said, "Check in with me before you go out…anywhere."

* * *

The rest of the weekend was uneventful, as were the first days at work the following week. On Wednesday, I learned a discon-certing fact from Dennis during a phone call. After telling me last Friday I could depend on police presence, his boss, Lieutenant Oliver, called off the surveillance. "I can still have a patrol car escort you to work and back; just not every day."

"What if Romeo kills someone tomorrow?" I said. "What if it's me?"

"Then I'll do everything to solve your murder."

I knew by his tone it was a joke, and he was doing his best to lighten the seriousness of the situation. I didn't appreciate the comment. I hung up.

Thursday night came and went. Still no bodies turned up that we could link to Romeo.

40

BY THE FOLLOWING THURSDAY, AGAIN THERE WERE no murders in Little Rock during the entire week. More than ten days since the newspaper article and no response or repercussions on that front. The blank card arrived a week and a half ago and I've heard nothing from Romeo. At any other time, I would consider the lull as a positive. I wondered what Romeo thought about the publicity. It seemed to have driven him underground. Even more, I wondered about the source of the story. Remembering Effie's comments regarding our neighbor, I was becoming more convinced Kenley Longstreet should be at the top of the list.

How should I approach him? I could go by myself and use a velvet glove technique. Including my roomies might be more intimidating and get better results. I needed Aaron and Effie's input. I'll talk to them tonight.

* * *

Over dinner, I made my proposal about approaching Kenley. A lot of haggling resolved itself to Aaron going alone. He reminded us that Kenley's lifestyle and his were compatible, and from day one our neighbor displayed an affinity for Aaron. "I think I can get him to open up."

"Don't offend him," I said. "If he leaked the information, we don't want to alienate him. We might be able to turn it to our advantage."

Aaron said, "You got it. I'll see if he's home now."

* * *

I heard Aaron at the front door returning when the phone rang. It was Dennis and his voice sounded excited. "I've got news about the last card," he said.

Aaron burst in and was standing inside the door—his eyes wide and he was doing a little dance. I've got two excited males—a spot I would, as a rule, enjoy—which should I choose first?

"Go ahead, Dennis."

"In the past all the cards came up clean, so I didn't put a rush on this one. The print lab just called me and guess what?"

"I don't know. It's snowing outside in May in Little Rock? Cut to the chase, Dennis."

There was a full print—a right thumb—on the card. Unfortunate for us, it belongs to Romeo's last murder victim." He paused as I related the facts to my roomies. He continued, "Here's the kicker." Dramatic pause…"There was another partial print on the postcard. It doesn't belong to the last victim or any of the other Vic's. Another downer—the print is not in any database, local, state or AFIS. Guy's never been printed."

I looked back at Aaron and gave him the latest info from Dennis. Aaron stopped his hip-hop dance, but now he was making wild gesturing motions toward our front door and pumping his head up and down. I was afraid he would injure himself.

Aaron said, "Tell Dennis, I think I have something that will blow your socks off."

I hung up the phone, promising to call back in a few minutes. "Did our guy screw up?" I said.

"This could be a big break," Aaron said.

41

AARON BLURTED OUT HIS WORDS AND GOT THE group's attention. "Kenley admitted he was the one who called the newspaper about our killer. He talked to them three times, but always from a different pay phone. The reporter doesn't know him and he is an 'anonymous' source."

"Doesn't seem like he knows enough to impress a reporter," Effie said. "Don't they demand more corroboration before writing a story?"

Aaron covered his conversation with Kenley. "He's seen us with at least two postcards—the one put in his box by accident and the one the night Raphael died. He remembers your cryptic comment when he saw your address on the card when he returned it. He also said he thought he could tie a murder to the cards he saw." Aaron stopped and took a breath. "I quizzed him about the messages on the cards—he remembers the two he saw but hasn't been able to make sense of them."

"Shouldn't be hard to shake the tree," I said. Pulling out the Sunday section in question, I looked below the caption, and the byline read: Yancy Haney. "I'll sick Dennis on him…Oh, I promised to call him back."

I explained the latest development to Dennis. As soon as he stopped sputtering about arresting my neighbor, I said, "Don't get your knickers in a twist. I think I have a way we can turn this to our advantage…but I don't know how to frame it."

"What are you talking about?"

"Seems to me our quarry has gone to ground. If nothing happens today, it'll be way over a week since the last killing. Maybe we can stage a leak to the press and flush him out."

"Come in first thing in the morning," Dennis said.

"I've been taking too much time off from work. Make it around five and I'll be there." He didn't disagree, so I tossed in, "I'm inviting Falcon as well." Again, no dissenting opinion and I signed off.

It took me a while to reach Falcon, but I told him about tonight and invited him to visit the police with me tomorrow. He said it would be fine, and I would see him in my rear view most of the time.

42

IT WAS CLOSE TO THE END OF THE DAY WHEN DENNIS showed up at my office. He turned my police "escort" loose, figuring he could shepherd me to his headquarters and then home. I was hopeful the trip would turn into a dinner date. Our relationship was in danger of floundering on the shoals and I wanted to bail out the leaking boat.

We were about to leave when Falcon arrived. "I thought you would meet us at the police station," I said. He shrugged and fell in behind us as we left.

Lieutenant Oliver was his usual charming self. Between grunts and growls, he looked at me and pointed to a chair. Guess that's as polite as he gets. His first words were, "Convince me why I shouldn't arrest that neighbor of yours."

I did my best to explain my idea. The fact I didn't have concrete details was like an anchor dragging on the bottom. "I'm not sure where to go…but the killer has slowed down or stopped. If we can't think of something to smoke him out, he may go to ground and we'll never catch him."

Dennis and Falcon agreed, but they faced the same dilemma—no firm action plan. Oliver took over again, "Ms. Fremont, you seem to have a good mind. Get to work on the problem and I'll give you the weekend to come up with a solution. If we don't have a plan by Tuesday, I'll have to arrest Mr. Longstreet." With that, the lieutenant got up and left the room.

"Wow, mighty big of him," I said. "The War Council will convene at my place at noon tomorrow. Bring a toothbrush and your jammies, 'cause no one leaves till we have a strategy to smoke Romeo out. And I'm not going to allow Kenley to go to jail."

Falcon nodded an agreement. Dennis on the other hand was frowning. I asked him if he talked to the reporter yet and he shook his head. I said, "If you're too busy to come tomorrow, at least give me the reporter's address as well as all his phone numbers." That he agreed to do.

* * *

My roomies and I set up a buffet lunch in the kitchen. I put pens and paper on the dining room table so we could work while we ate. Becca arrived at a quarter to twelve with Falcon and Dennis following close behind. Everyone loaded a plate and took either coffee or tea to the table. The first stabs at conversation were unsuccessful due to mouths full of food. We opted to forgo the discussion and settled on making notes until the plates were empty.

As I ate, I scratched questions on my legal pad.

1) What does he want?

2) What will bring him out in the open?

3) What can we use for bait?

4) How will we get the information to him?

5) Can we lure him to a specific location?

Everyone pitched in to clean our eating area. Returning from the kitchen, we all took our seats around the table. I decided to start the ball rolling. "Let's all share whatever notes we made during lunch. Brainstorming rules apply, no arguments or comments." I looked to my right and said, "Falcon, please start and we'll go around the table."

During Dennis' turn, Aaron started to say something. I held up my hand. "Remember, no evaluations. If you have a comment, make a note of it and bring it up after everyone has their chance to speak."

When it was my turn, I read the five questions I scribbled earlier. I said, "Aaron, go ahead with the comment you started to make earlier."

Aaron said, "Dennis was stressing we need to draw Romeo out. Sounded a little like staking out a goat in the middle of the jungle…could be dangerous for the goat."

After everyone exercised their chance to comment, Falcon said, "I think all our comments are embodied in the questions Casey listed. Seems obvious he wants her. I'm afraid Casey will have to be the goat—the bait. I doubt we can lure him anywhere not of his own choosing. And…how we get the information to him seems simple enough."

With that, Falcon stopped speaking and took a sip of water. I admired his flair for the dramatic. He left us all hanging, wanting more. I didn't have anything to add. Nor did the others at the table.

When the silence was unbearable, he continued, "The perfect vehicle for dissemination of information is the newspaper reporter who has already involved herself in the story."

"The reporter's a woman?" Aaron said.

Falcon smiled. "Didn't take much digging to learn a good deal about Yancy Haney. Do you want her fax, her cell phone number or home address?"

"Okay," Aaron said. "We know a lot about her, what's the next step?"

Effie said, "If we can get her to go along, maybe we can plant a story that could help us draw Romeo out of his shell."

During the following discussion, Dennis offered that we could threaten her and ease her pain at the same time. He said, "Maybe she'll be satisfied if we promise an exclusive when the capture is imminent."

Falcon reached for his water glass again and said, "Can you guarantee the offer, Dennis?" When Dennis nodded an affirmative, Falcon continued, "Then I think we should formulate a scenario that will not scare him off."

We also decided to bring Kenley Longstreet into our group and hope we could trust him. If he violated our trust, we could be in worse shape than we are now. We needed a time and a place—and a setup that would intrigue Romeo. If he got a whiff of anything out of the ordinary, he would bolt down his rabbit's hole—possibly never to be seen again.

* * *

By noon on Sunday, I received word from Dennis. Lieutenant Oliver would extend our deadline until close of business on Tuesday. He also told me a discussion with the lieutenant and an assistant district attorney gave us a go-ahead to promise the newspaper columnist an exclusive if she cooperated with us.

Now, all we needed to do was concoct a story for her to print, get her to agree to go along with us, and have Kenley Longstreet back us up with her. All? The more I thought about it, the bigger the chore sounded.

Becca left last night and was due back by one p.m. today, as was Falcon. Dennis would sit this session out. Aaron, Effie and I finished a quick lunch and cleaned up the dining room table to be ready for our working group. If we didn't have an acceptable scenario by today, we might be too late to make the Monday late edition of the paper. We were hoping to get the ball rolling before the holiday weekend was over.

As our meeting progressed, we came to the conclusion the newspaper story didn't need to hit the streets as soon as we first thought. It might even be best to hold off and be sure we could set the hook well. We would need to bring Kenley in and update him. We felt the reporter would be more comfortable hearing his voice. On top of that, Dennis would have to convince her she could have an exclusive by playing along. When those steps were done, we would have to feed her the story. It was beginning to look like it would be Wednesday or Thursday before the article could hit the streets.

With logistical planning behind us, we turned to the actual story and the imbedded hook. It took us an hour before we were done developing and polishing the article. It was time to enlist Kenley's help.

43

AARON REACHED KENLEY LONGSTREET ON THE
phone and convinced him to come over to my apartment. "He's
nervous about coming," Aaron said. "I think he's afraid we are
mad at him for the first article about the Postcard Killer."

Kenley arrived and I assured him he wasn't in any trouble.
Quite the contrary, he could be of invaluable help and in on the
conclusion of the case. Thirty minutes later, he knew almost as
much as we did about the murderer and the killings.

After a short break, Falcon began tracking down the reporter,
Yancy Haney. He called her home phone, her cell and tried the
switchboard at the newspaper. None of these produced imme-
diate results. He sent a short note by fax asking her to return his
calls. The words "cooperation" and "exclusive" were featured in
his communications. We sat back and waited.

I was surprised when Falcon's phone rang fifteen minutes
later. We could tell he was talking to the reporter. He must have
used the word "exclusive" a half-dozen times or more. He waved
Kenley over, saying into the phone, "I'm sure you'll recognize
the voice which gave you the first story."

Kenley spoke for a few minutes and handed the phone back.

Falcon listened on the phone for a moment, then said to
the reporter, "You need to speak to Detective Sergeant Dennis
Epstein. He can confirm an exclusive story in return for your
cooperation." He listened again. "No, it's not going to work that
way. We have a story we want you to print, but…you don't get
it until you're satisfied with the terms and we have your word as
well." He gave her Dennis' phone numbers and hung up.

Falcon said to the rest of us, "If she can get a confirmation, she's on board. The idea of being in on the arrest of a multiple killer is too much to turn down."

"What's the story you want me to give Yancy?" Kenley said.

I didn't know how to let my neighbor down. During our earlier discussions, the group decided Falcon should handle getting our story to the reporter. I breathed a sigh of relief when Falcon stood and walked toward Kenley.

Falcon reached out and shook the old man's hand. "We appreciate all you've done up to now. I think we better handle the rest ourselves. The fewer people we have involved, the fewer people will be in danger. And I think we all agree that the level of the threat will rise with this step."

Kenley looked like all the air was just sucked out of him. Taking in a deep breath, he gathered himself and left. I thought I noticed a difference in his walk and his shoulders slumping more than usual.

Waiting for callbacks from Yancy and Dennis was fruitless. We plowed our way through Chinese food delivery and cleaned the table. Falcon and Becca decided to call it quits. I invited everyone to reconvene tomorrow morning. Being a holiday, no one would be going to work. I left a message on Dennis' voice mail and invited him over as well.

* * *

Monday morning came and went. Becca and Falcon arrived to join us for lunch, but no word from the police or the reporter. At one o'clock, both my home phone and cell rang at the same time. I grabbed the phone, checked caller ID and asked the reporter to hold and answered my cell. Dennis told me he confirmed the go-ahead from his lieutenant and a district attorney. I relayed the information to Yancy Haney. I told Dennis to get his buns over to my place and hung up. It took a bit of doing, but I convinced Yancy to come to my home.

When the doorbell rang, I checked the peephole and saw Dennis standing there with a woman I didn't recognize. As the two walked in, I sized up the female I assumed was the reporter, Yancy Haney. She walked ahead of Dennis—was good looking with shoulder length auburn hair—was a little shorter in stature than me, and she walked like she wanted others to notice her body. It was worth noticing, and I caught Dennis appreciating his view of her backside. Yancy also has one of those hair habits I hate. On her trip into the living room, she tucked her hair behind an ear—twice.

I invited Yancy to sit at the dining room table. She declined anything to drink and pulled a pad and a small recorder from a voluminous shoulder bag. I looked at Falcon. He put his hand on top of the recorder and said, "No recordings." He also slid the notepad out of her reach.

Before she could object, I introduced Yancy to everyone and turned the meeting back to Falcon. He said, "What I'm going to cover next is on deep background. It cannot be quoted or released in any fashion until the case is concluded. Do you understand and accept the terms?"

Yancy agreed and tucked hair behind an ear. I fought off the desire to reach out and slap her hand. Falcon continued, "That's good, because if you violate our trust, I want you to know there are things in life worse than losing a job over a source."

The reporter looked impressed and somewhat intimidated by this man dressed in black sitting next to her. She pointed to her notepad and Falcon shook his head. She leaned back and turned in her chair toward him.

Falcon covered the story about Romeo from the first postcard up to today. He didn't go into the minutia, but I was surprised how much detail he included. The description of Becca's driving when we chased Romeo and were targets raised a few goose bumps on my arms. The last item he covered was Romeo's phone call to me. He produced a recorder and let Yancy listen to the words. When the recording ended, Falcon snapped the little machine off, looked at the reporter and cocked his head.

Yancy leaned forward and said, "What's the story you want me to tell?"

Falcon produced a folded sheet of paper from an inside jacket pocket. "I've noted the salient points to include," he said. "I want you to write it in your own words. Our killer is no dummy, and he might recognize a change in style if someone else composes it."

Yancy said, "Do you want to see it before it hits the street?"

"What day do you expect the story will appear?" Falcon said.

"I'll write it tonight, do my review in the morning and send a copy to you by noon. If you can get it right back to me, I should be able to talk my boss into running it and make the deadline for Wednesday morning's paper."

Yancy and Falcon settled on details for the editing process. Yancy closed with, "This will be fun to write. But…I'm looking forward to the big exposé at the end. We've got an ironclad deal, haven't we?" She looked at Dennis.

Dennis squirmed in his seat, and said, "Even if a higher-up reneges, you can bank on a call from me so you can be there when we take him down."

The reporter stood. "How much can I tell my boss if this turns into a hard sell?"

Falcon said, "You can tell him the police will give you exclusive coverage on later events. You may not tell him the story about Casey is fabricated. If this plan goes south, I want a limited number of people I can point a finger toward."

* * *

Tuesday at work, I thought back to the three-day weekend. We did some good work. I wondered how long it would be before Falcon called. I went back to my legal research, but it didn't take my mind off the story. Being the sacrificial lamb was unsettling. We all agreed, even me, this was our best chance of smoking Romeo out.

Tuesday went, as well as most of Wednesday. I dialed Falcon's number several times with no answer. Back on Monday, he promised to call as soon as the story was going to print. My period of vulnerability would start as soon as the article hit the streets.

I was on my way home when my cell rang. Pulling to the shoulder I saw it was Falcon and answered.

"Casey, it's all set," he said. "I reviewed the story details and the reporter's editor gave a go-ahead. He was the stumbling block, but your story will be in tomorrow morning's paper."

"I suppose I'm relieved. At least we're on the last leg. Can I expect to see you tomorrow?"

"I'll have a second person. Dennis also has two detectives assigned. We'll work in pairs. My guy and I will be there tomorrow morning. The two cops will take over in the evening. I've already put photos of my assistant and the two policemen in your mailbox. See you in the a.m."

He was gone, leaving me to my images of what might happen tomorrow.

44

EARLY THURSDAY MORNING ROMEO SETTLED IN AT a table in one of his favorite coffee shops. As soon as his computer was set up and connected to the wireless network, he called up the local newspaper on his browser and logged on.

Scrolling down the headlines, one caught his eye. He maneuvered his mouse pointer over the link to the story and gave the left-click button on his laptop a vicious stab.

When the page appeared on his monitor, he leaned forward to read it.

Post Card Killer May Be Caught Short

BY YANCY HANEY

Since the first story I wrote two and a half weeks ago about the Post Card Killer (PCK), additional sources have come forward and provided details of the killings and that the target of the PCK's attention may leave the city, neutering his pathetic attempts to impress this woman.

I was given unprecedented access to several principals, including the target and a police detective, involved in this bizarre tale. While many details cannot be disclosed, many aspects like: Romeo's description (yes, PCK dubbed himself Romeo), the exact number of his killings or how close the police investigation is to identifying the murderer.

It can be reported—of the postcards PCK, or Romeo, sent to the target of his attentions—ALL contained cryptic messages and images. When decoded, the words turned out to be clues to a killing and that the murders were patterned after deaths in well-known fictional detective or mystery stories.

Here's why I say PCK may be "caught short." When I spoke to the lady who is the target, she seemed nervous and upset. She talked of taking a vacation—"two to four weeks," she said. Reading between the lines, I got the impression her move might be permanent. She refused to even hint at a destination, saying, "It won't be anywhere I could be connected to." When asked about the timing of the trip, she deferred. An open door to her bedroom revealed suitcases on her bed. I would say that her flight is imminent.

A move like this will leave PCK/Romeo without a target to impress—and all his efforts wasted. At this point I have no idea whether there will ever be another installment in this series.

Romeo closed his laptop and left the shop. He fished two quarters from his pocket and purchased a copy of the newspaper from a vending machine on the sidewalk. He hurried home and looked at the paper for the first time. Above the masthead, he read: Postcard Killer May Be Caught Short…story on 2A.

As he read and reread the words on the newsprint, Romeo felt his face flush and he clenched his fists. He leaned back, closed his eyes and began an audible hum. At last he sat up and thought, I have a lot of work to do in a short time…planning will be critical. Romeo bolted upright with a snap of his fingers. He said to an empty room, "Now, that is a plan to confound them all."

45

TODAY'S THE DAY. THE THURSDAY MORNING PAPER
should be out by now, and I was the bait in the cage. I padded
around my home eating a bite of breakfast, if you can call Pop-
Tarts breakfast, and leaving more than I finished. Aaron and Effie
kept ducking out of my way and generally being pains in the ass.

I need to cut them some slack. I know they're worried about
me and don't know what to say. After several silent passes by
one another, I cornered them both in the kitchen. "Okay, you
two. Stop creeping around like the floor is covered with eggs."
No replies. "C'mon. I'm nervous too but acting like mutes won't
help." A few minutes of light banter and I felt much better and
started for my room to get ready for work. Stepping out of my
shower, I heard the doorbell ring. Figuring one of my roomies
would answer it, I continued to towel dry. Seconds later, the bell
rang again—this time several insistent rings indicating someone
was leaning on the button.

Uttering a mild oath, I wrapped the towel around me and
made my way to the front door. Through the peephole, I saw
Falcon and a brunette I didn't recognize. He made the introductions and Inger Johansen reached out to shake hands. I noticed
that except for the hair color, we might have passed for sisters.
Falcon explained the plan for today and Inger and I retired to
my room. Thirty-minutes later we went back to the living room.
By now Inger was the blonde and I was a brunette. She was
wearing some of my clothes and we were sporting the wigs she
brought with her.

Falcon's plan included Inger driving the Mustang to my job

with Falcon trailing behind. Forrest Benton, the other fellow helping Falcon on this part of the caper, would also ride along with us. Inger would go inside the law office building while Falcon and I slipped in the back. Inside, we planned to execute a restroom role-reversal—I was to head for my work and Inger would go out back to join Benton. Falcon could hang around the building to keep an eye on me. Since he worked for the Peligrier Agency, it shouldn't arouse suspicion. After work, the reversal of roles again in order to get me home.

This was the first time I've seen Falcon when he was "working." His head swiveled without stop and he muttered comments and questions to himself. He also kept up a running commentary with Inger via a handheld radio.

When Inger pulled into the parking garage at work, he spoke into his mike, "Heads up. If he's going to hit, this would be the logical place."

"Roger that," Inger said.

Falcon let Benton out so he could cover Inger and we took the back stairs to the law offices.

* * *

I was surprised when I looked up and my desk clock read eleven-oh-five. At almost the same time a shadow fell across my cubical. I started because I didn't hear anyone approach. Looking up, I expected to see Falcon. Instead, it was Vince; the creepy son of the Peligrier Agency's owner. I did my best to bury my head back in my research and pretend I didn't see him. Too late.

Vince plopped himself down in the chair next to my desk and looked like he was settling in for a long winter's nap. I smiled at my own humor and Vince took it for a greeting. He launched into a long-winded explanation of why he was here. None of it made sense and I was convinced he didn't have anything better to do.

"Vince, I'm pretty busy. If you have any business for me, let's get to it. Otherwise, I'll have to say good-bye."

He got all huffy. At least as huffy as Vince could get, which wasn't very impressive. He got up, muttered a couple of "damns" and stalked off saying, "I know when I'm not wanted…but I'll be back."

The cursing was a surprise. I never heard him use coarse language before. And…he appeared to be angry when he left—an emotion I never saw from him before.

"Sorry I didn't warn you," Falcon said.

"Damn, where did you come from?"

Without explaining, Falcon said, "He slipped by me. I must be getting old or senile—or both. He's a sneaky shit; I'll give him that."

We arranged for take-out delivery for lunch, so there was no need to leave the building until it was time to go home. Inger drove my car while Falcon followed her with Benton and me in his car.

The two police officers took the night shift and reported "all quiet" to Falcon in the morning.

Friday was a repeat of the previous day and no sightings of any bad guys. We conducted a war council meeting in the evening. I asked Falcon for his thoughts as to why Romeo was lying low.

"I think we caught him short," Falcon said. "It appears he likes to allow time to get ready for his next adventure. In the past, he liked to kill on a Thursday, which gave him a minimum of a week for planning. Probably much more because I think he forms his plans well in advance."

Becca said, "Do you think he'll wait until next week to make a move?"

Falcon shook his head. "I doubt it. The story in the paper leaves no doubt Casey is leaving soon."

"What if he doesn't make a move this weekend?" I said.

Falcon shook his head again. This time he didn't say anything.

46

THE POLICEMEN ASSIGNED TO US ARRIVED FOR THE night shift and Falcon evaporated. One minute he was there and the next he was gone. Inger Johansen disappeared at the same time, and I assumed he would drop her at home. She was due back Sunday night so we could resume the ruse if need be. The late evening news was on when my phone rang. It was Falcon. He said, "Have any of you heard from Yancy Haney?"

I told him we didn't know her whereabouts. He detailed a call to him from her newspaper editor. No one at the paper heard from her since late Thursday afternoon. They tried to reach her all day today with no results. Falcon added, "Her editor says she always checks in several times a day to see if anything new is in the wind. Casey, I've got a bad feeling about this."

"Not very reassuring," I said.

"I know. Check the cops outside your place. Better yet, send Aaron."

I was moving toward my bedroom when I said, "Won't be necessary. By the time I get to the front door, Romeo would have to be faster than a speeding bullet to get me." I propped the phone in the crook of my neck as I retrieved my Glock and loaded it. I racked the slide back to put a shell into the chamber and a voice came from the phone. "What the hell was that?" Falcon said.

I explained, went to the front door and checked the peephole. I saw nothing. Where the hell are the cops? I was about to panic when the elevator doors slid open and a police officer came out. Opening my door, I motioned him inside. I gave him my phone so Falcon could explain the situation. The cop produced a cell

phone, checked with his partner and assured Falcon and me all
was quiet. He resumed his station outside my condo. Falcon said
Dennis was aware of Yancy's disappearance. I said goodnight to
Falcon and stored the gun back in my room.

* * *

I hate it when the phone rings before the sun is up, especially
on a Saturday morning. I rubbed my eyes and looked at the
clock—four fifty-seven.

Falcon apologized for the early call. "I just hung up with
Dennis. He has an unidentified female body…it could be Inger."

All I could say was, "Damn."

"Casey, I'm going down to the morgue to help ID her. My guy
Benton is on his way to your place. Stay inside…out of sight. I'll
come over as soon as I can."

I started a pot of coffee and picked up the paper from outside
my front door. Sipping coffee and riffling through the pages of
the paper, I waited while the hands of the kitchen clock slogged
toward eight a.m.

Aaron stumbled in and reached for the coffee. I jumped up.
"Sit down before you spill the whole pot. I'll pour."

I was explaining Falcon's call when Effie put in an appearance.
I caught them both up and said, "Either of you know where
Yancy is?" They shook their heads and I reached for my phone.
It took fifteen minutes to call all the numbers listed for her in
my notes and leave a message at each location. "I wonder how
long it'll take Falcon to call back." I looked at my roomies and
said, "I sure hope it's not Inger."

Effie said, "Me too. I only met her once, but I really liked her."

As if on cue, my phone rang and caller ID announced Falcon.
I snatched it up and punched the TALK button.

"Bad news, Casey," Falcon said. "Inger is dead." He gave me
time to gather myself before he continued. "Looks like she went

quick…strangled…no other obvious marks or bruising. No indi-
cation of sexual assault. And…not a sign of forensic evidence.
Damn. I don't know how he identified and found her…but I'd
bet big money it's Romeo's work."

Fidgeting and folding a page corner of the paper, I said, "What
makes you so sure?"

"She was dumped in the middle of an area where prostitutes
work. The lack of physical evidence screams Romeo."

I tore off the dog-eared corner and waited to see if he would
add to his observations. He didn't and I said, "Did he think it
was me?"

"Doubt it," Falcon said. "He must have been hanging close
all day Thursday and Friday. I can't see it, but it's the only explanation for how he got to her so quick. The M.E. estimated her
death at around midnight and lividity indicates she was dumped
later…best guess is about three this morning."

"I'm not feeling good about this," I said. "In fact, I'm damned
shaky."

Falcon said, "Hang in there, Casey. "I'm on my way to your
place and we can work out our next steps."

* * *

Becca arrived within twenty-five minutes of my call to her
and Falcon was a few minutes behind her. She and my roomies
gathered to hear Falcon's plans.

Falcon outlined his ideas, which included moving me to a
"safe" house.

"Where is it?" I said.

Shaking his head, Falcon said, "As much as I trust all of you,
I'm keeping the location to myself."

I wanted my roomies to come along, but Falcon nixed the
idea saying, "If everyone is gone from here, it could be a tip off
and we don't need that." He looked around and added, "It's okay
with me if you want Becca to join us."

I looked at Becca and she nodded an assent. I said, "I suppose taking my car along is out of the question too."

"Well, if we do, might as well park a fire-engine red beast in the driveway and shoot off flares to attract attention."

"I'll take that for a no."

47

ROMEO SMILED AS HE WATCHED YANCY.

* * *

Yancy Haney struggled behind the blindfold. The haze was beginning to fade, and she concentrated all her energy to bring her mind into the present. How damn long have I been here? She could remember being grabbed from behind when she arrived at her car in the newspaper's parking lot. She could remember the stinging pain in her neck and slumping into oblivion. The next memory she could dredge up was being restrained in this hard, wooden chair and the questions. From the smell and taste, Yancy assumed it was Duct Tape holding her arms and legs to the chair as well as forming a gag and blindfold.

He, whoever he was, repeated the questions. The endless questions about the article she wrote for the paper and about Casey Fremont. The man kept shouting: Where is she going? When is she leaving? Her mind went back to the conversation with Falcon. What was it they called him? Romeo? Could this be the man they were after?

The man lowered his voice and almost in a whisper, said, "This is the last time I am going to ask. If you do not begin cooperating, I will be forced to inflict pain—exquisite pain."

Yancy squirmed in the chair and against the gag. How the hell can I cooperate, buster, with my mouth taped shut? She muttered words against the tape, but they made no sense even to her. What happens if I tell him the truth? Once he gets the details out of me, my life isn't worth a cent. He'll kill me in a New York minute. How much pain can I endure? Maybe I can stand it long enough to make a lie seem like the truth.

"I am going to tell you a secret," Romeo said.

Yancy twisted toward the voice and hoped he would go easy if she seemed attentive. It didn't work. The man smacked her on the side of the face with an open hand, and she tasted blood in her mouth.

"You are the first to know I killed Inger Johansen. You know… the person pretending to be Casey Fremont. I finished her off last night and tossed her body out in the worst neighborhood I could think of. I am sure she told the truth—could not resist the pain she went through."

Yancy concentrated and did her best to clear her head. Even behind the blindfold, the room was spinning. How long has he kept me here? Grabbed me on Friday…I'm sure it must be Saturday by now…could it be Sunday? Don't think so, but how late on Saturday is it? Please, let someone be looking for me …

The hand slap to the other side of her face caught her off guard. She snorted as she drew a deep breath in through her nose.

"If you are ready to talk with me, you can nod your head."

Yancy played for more time and held her head still.

The double slap, one to each side of her head, set the spinning room in motion again. "Now my dear, let us not play hard to get. Are you ready to talk with me?"

Through a building haze, she nodded. Fingers ripped the tape from her mouth. "Please may I have a drink?" she said.

Romeo slapped her before retreating for a glass of water. When he returned, he said, "Do not take me for a fool, my dear. Trivial ploys to buy time like this will not work in your favor. Every minute you waste will expand the pain level you will endure. Now drink."

Yancy sipped at the glass which was pressed to her lips. Bastard, she thought. He's put salt in the damn water to make me thirstier. May help me yet. The salt will help the cuts on the inside of my mouth.

"Could I please have the tape off my eyes," she said.

"Oh, no. If you see my face, I will have to kill you. As it is, I will let you go free as soon as you tell me what I need to know."

Two more blows rained down on her and she heard the sound of his Taser hissing a few inches from her face.

Oh, Lord, give me the strength, she thought.

48

IT TOOK ME LONGER TO PACK AND PREPARE TO MOVE
out than Falcon would have liked. The scowls and grunts were
enough to tell me he wasn't pleased. I said, "Couldn't we wait
until tomorrow to make the break? The traffic's a lot lighter on
Sunday morning."

Falcon turned his attention to Becca. "I suppose you need to
go home before we can get on the road."

"All I need to do is grab a small suitcase from the trunk of
my car," Becca said.

When we reached Falcon's car, I was disappointed. He
unlocked the door to a Toyota Celica, which looked like it was
on its last legs. Looks were deceiving. The tires appeared brand-
new, the stick shifter wasn't stock and when he started the engine,
it was easy to tell the purr was from a large V-8. Becca and
I squeezed into the backseat while Benton rode on the front
passenger side. I watched between the two front seat backs as
Falcon maneuvered out of the parking lot and ran the little car
through the gears. It looked like the transmission was at least
a five-speed.

I looked at Becca and said, "Bet this is a fun one to drive."
She nodded her head and grinned.

Falcon took us around most of the city of Little Rock before
we ended back on the west side of town. All the while, he and
Benton kept an eye on their mirrors and twisted in their seats
for better views of neighborhoods we passed through. He eased
into the on-ramp lane, downshifted and smashed the accelera-
tor. We rocketed along, southbound in the left lane. At the last

moment, he cut the wheel hard to the right and hit the exit ramp for Colonel Glenn Road. He did a hard left at the intersection and stayed on the street past the junction with Asher Avenue where he turned north. A couple of more jinks in the residential neighborhood and he took a northbound route.

We were a few miles south of our starting point. He circled the same block twice before pulling into the driveway of a small bungalow. Maneuvering onto the grass behind the house, he did a Y-turn and backed into the detached, oversize garage. It was nearly dark by now, but I could see a well-stocked auto repair area.

Becca was staring out the back window as well and said, "Don't suppose you'll give us a tour of this here shop?" When Falcon shook his head, she said, "How 'bout letting me take a spin in this little beauty?" She seemed to take his silence as a no and struggled out of the rear seat.

At the back of the house was a low slanted entrance abutting the foundation. When Falcon opened the door, the sound was that of metal even though the paint made it look like wood. A flight of steps led to the basement and two large metal bars secured the entrance once we were inside. "Wouldn't it have been easier to use the regular doors?" I said.

Falcon grunted. "There are some nasty surprises inside the front and back doors. I'll show you, then you best stay clear of them."

Becca and I would be sharing a bedroom at the back of the house. were Burglar-bars covered the outside of the window and heavy black drapes hung inside. I figured the room would be in total darkness at night with the lights out. We each dumped our possessions into a single dresser drawer and placed three hangers apiece in the closet. The clothes looked lonesome, mine hanging to the right and Becca's on the left.

Before we sat down to eat, Falcon pointed out the trip wires at the main entrances to the house. "What do they trip?" I said.

He lifted the hem of a lightweight drape by the front door and revealed a heavy spring attached to a steel bar. "If anyone sets off the trigger, the spring propels the bar in an arc and whacks the person in the shins about twelve inches off the floor. If it doesn't break a leg, it should incapacitate them for quite a while."

"Why not attach the wire to a gun?" Becca said.

"Too much damn paperwork and legal hurdles to negotiate when you shoot someone." Hefting a sawed-off baseball bat, he said, "Fractured legs and concussions are way easier to explain."

After the meal, Becca and I cleared the table. I started for the back door with the trash and thought better of it. I asked Benton what to do with it and he pointed to a large can with a lock-lid. "Put it in there. Don't want accumulation outside. People might think the place is occupied." He turned and left the kitchen.

"Man of few words," I said to Becca.

She gave me a shoulder shrug. "I think I'll take a nap. Any preference which twin you want?"

I followed her to the bedroom and she took the one nearest the window. I laid down on the other one but knew I wouldn't be able to sleep. Becca's snoring let me know she wasn't fazed by our situation. I woke with a start and was surprised I was able to sleep. I rolled over and Morpheus wrapped his arms around me again.

* * *

The next time I stirred, the light was bright in the room—neither one of us thought to turn off the overhead light last night. I looked toward Becca's bed and found she was gone. I flipped over and slid out of bed. Even before I got to the living room, I heard Falcon's voice. He was on his cell phone and used Yancy's name. Another few seconds confirmed he was talking to her. She was alive, and I was elated.

Benton appeared from the back of the house carrying a large Sunday newspaper. Falcon looked at Benton. "Lock up behind you?" Benton nodded his head. Falcon said, "See anything unusual while you were out in the neighborhood?" A head shake was the answer. Falcon went back to the phone.

We heard Falcon give some whispered directions. He folded his phone, slipped it into a pocket and said, "Yancy is on her way here. Benton…make sure everything is ready. She'll be here in a half hour or so and we can expect other visitors after that."

I was sure Falcon was referring to Romeo. With a sense of dread, goose bumps covered my body.

49

FALCON DISARMED THE TRIP WIRE AND EASED OUT the front door. He moved toward the sidewalk and stood beside a large tree in the yard. We watched through gaps in the closed drapes. Even in the daylight, Falcon almost blended into the front yard scenery.

After a short wait, a car pulled to the curb and Yancy Haney emerged. Falcon looked both directions, then took her by the arm. They moved across the yard at a rapid pace and climbed the steps to the front porch. Benton jerked the door open and the two entered the living room without breaking stride. Falcon reset the trip and we all gathered around Yancy peppering her with questions.

Falcon held up his hands palms out and everyone fell silent. "Yancy, do you need anything to eat or drink?"

"I could use some water," she said.

Becca and I stumbled over one another and returned with a large tumbler of ice and water.

Falcon allowed time for her to drink before saying, "Tell us the story from the beginning."

Yancy began with her abduction from the newspaper parking lot on Friday and went step-by-step through her escape this morning.

Falcon said, "Go into all the detail about your escape and getting here."

"I worked on the tape around my wrists all last night. He took off the tape on my right hand so I could eat some food he brought. I twisted my arm as he re-taped me and when I twisted my arm later there was a little slack. I kept pulling and twisting until I got the hand free. I was afraid he'd be sitting there watching me when I pulled the blindfold off…but he wasn't." She squirmed in her seat and shivered as she related the escape from the chair. "His voice was distinctive and I think I could recognize it if I heard it again."

Her experience was obvious. There were several bruises on her cheeks and one eye was puffed up to the point it must have obscured her vision.

The ice clinked in the glass as she took several sips. Yancy continued her story. "The door to the room was locked, but the dead bold operated from the inside. I don't think he expected me to get loose from the tape."

Falcon interrupted. "How close to your office were you being held?"

Yancy seemed surprised by the question. "It was only about five blocks."

"Let's not sell Romeo short," Falcon said. "I would wager a considerable sum he left the tape loose on purpose. I also think he was watching your escape via a peephole or closed-circuit TV. My bet would include the fact he followed you to your car as well."

"Well, he didn't follow me here." Yancy stood with a hand on her hip. "I'm damn good at spotting a tail."

"I'm sure you are," Falcon said. "He probably put a GPS bug in your car while he was holding you. All he needed to confirm was the fact you used your own car."

"I could find the place where he held me," she said. "Oh, and I found these before I left." She reached into a pocket in her slacks and produced a pair of green surgical scrubs booties.

"He wore the same things when he kidnapped me," I said.

Falcon took the booties. "That's part of his M.O. Helps keep him from leaving trace evidence behind. Wonder what he does with the scrubs later."

"Hey, wait a minute," Becca said. "If Romeo knows where we are, why the hell aren't we getting out of here?"

"Because," Falcon said, "this is what I want. When Yancy called, I expected Romeo would follow. Now I'm sure he did and we'll be waiting for him."

* * *

The sun was in the final part of its daily arc. "How damn long do we have to wait?" I said.

"Be patient, Casey," Falcon said. "Waiting is part of his game. He hopes we'll get jumpy and then complacent. I rather imagine he'll be here a bit after dark."

Falcon flipped a wall switch and explained it controlled motion sensors around the house. He pointed to a small box with several little lights. "The top row represents the front yard and the bottom row covers the back."

The sun was down and only the last vestiges of daylight remained. I was doing my best to prepare for a long wait when a faint glow from the warning box caught my attention.

Falcon whispered, "The lights indicate the front walk and porch."

50

FALCON AND BENTON EACH HELD A GUN. I THOUGHT about the Glock in my purse, but it was in the bedroom. The draw of the unknown outside was too strong and I moved to the window looking out on the porch. Before Falcon could pull me aside, I eased the edge of the drape away from the window. My mouth dropped open at what I saw. Standing on the porch was a tall gentleman with gray hair looking confused. He was punching the doorbell button and nothing was happening.

"My God," I said. "It's my neighbor, Kenley Longstreet."

I disarmed the trip wire and was reaching for the doorknob when Falcon grabbed my arm.

"Stand back," he said. "I'll let him in."

Kenley's confused expression gave way to surprise and fear as he saw two men menacing him with weapons. Falcon reached forward and jerked the old man through the door. He held Kenley with a firm grip while Benton closed and locked the door then reset the trip. Next Benton patted Longstreet down and when he got to the ankles I think we all noticed the old man was wearing green surgical booties over his shoes. Benton rose and announced, "He's clean."

Falcon stepped in front of Kenley, shoved him in the chest and shouted, "How the hell did you get here?"

I was afraid my old neighbor would have a heart attack, so I stepped between the two of them. I used my softest voice. "Kenley, how did you get here?"

He told of finding an envelope outside his door. Someone rang his bell but disappeared before he could get there. He found a note and the booties inside. "Casey, the instructions gave this address and said you were in trouble…and since it was a crime scene I should wear these things over my shoes."

"Where's the note?" Falcon said in his usual accusatory tone.

"I tossed it and the envelope into the incinerator chute."

"Why?" Falcon said.

"Ah…the note told me to do it."

"And you always do what notes say?"

I turned on Falcon. "Ease up." I led Kenley to a chair and he sagged into it. "Do you realize how suspicious this all looks?" I said to him.

We talked to Longstreet and questioned him. His story never varied and I believed him. From Falcon's tone and questions, I think he was still skeptical, but there was little any of us could do except wait for something to happen or someone else to appear.

We settled in for the night. Benton and Falcon took shifts so someone was awake all night. Kenley used the sofa, Becca and I tossed and turned for most of the night, but I think she slept some. I did.

The morning sunlight woke me and I found everyone in the living room. The table was stacked with egg and sausage breakfast sandwiches. I learned Benton just returned from a nearby fast-food drive-through. By early afternoon, Falcon decided our plan wasn't working. He took me aside. "Be damn careful when we get back to your place. I'm still not certain your neighbor is innocent."

I said, "I can't imagine this old gay man is capable of killing all those people."

"Don't be deceived by appearances. Under those clothes I think the old guy is in pretty good physical condition…and he's not as old as he wants everyone to believe."

We packed our meager belongings into bags and made our way out of the house through the basement. Wedged into the backseat of the dark red Celica, I felt drained. Ever since we left my place Saturday, I was pumped up and on edge. Now it was over, but it really wasn't over yet. Romeo was still out there—somewhere. And we didn't have the faintest idea where he was or what he was planning.

Becca and I were both in the back, and the front passenger seat was empty. I used my cell phone to let my roomies know we were on our way home. Benton was with Yancy. A radio crackled, "Falcon, Benton here." Falcon acknowledged the call and the other man said, "Found the tracker. It ain't trackin' no more. We're right behind you." Falcon clicked the transmit button twice and laid the handheld back down on the seat.

Becca leaned forward and said, "What's next, Sherlock?"

I jabbed her with an elbow.

"Do I detect a note of sarcasm?" Falcon said.

It was my turn. "I think Becca is feeling like me, frustrated. We were all set to end this and now… "

"Guys like Romeo come from both ends of the intelligence continuum," Falcon said. "It's our bad luck he's on the high IQ end of the scale. He's sharp, a good planner and hard to stay ahead of."

Back in my condo parking garage, Falcon swung into a visitor's slot. Yancy pulled into a parking place two cars away. She and Benton joined us. Kenley arrived a few minutes later and met us by the elevator. Falcon tossed the car keys to Benton and told him to return around midnight. Benton watched as Falcon waved his hands in front of him, then left in the Celica.

"What was that with the hands?" I said to Falcon.

"Mostly American Sign Language with some variations."

I led the way up to my home. When we reached the eighth floor, I looked at Kenley and said, "I'll see you later."

He turned toward his door and entered without saying a word. When I unlocked my own door, Aaron and Effie pounced on us, the questions coming so fast I couldn't make them out. Aaron set an extra place at the table for Yancy and we settled in while

Effie served the meal she put together after I called. Referring to the meal prep, I said, "This lady's talents never cease to amaze me." Effie blushed and returned to the kitchen.

A few bites of food and we calmed down. I recounted our experiences at the safe-house, omitting details of the trip wires and surveillance equipment. Falcon nodded his head and smiled. I tried to remember if I ever saw him smile before. Yancy told the others about her period of captivity to mostly open-mouth gawks.

Aaron said, "You don't really think Kenley could be Romeo, do you? I mean he's such a sweet old guy."

Everyone added a comment, but it came back to Falcon's analysis—the old man wasn't as old as he appeared and he also was in better physical shape than he let on.

There was a streak of bluish-gray fur racing for the living room. The sight and the resulting thud got Yancy's attention. "What in the world was that?"

"That's my cat, PK," I said. "Stands for Psycho Kitty and he bounces off the living room wall on a regular basis." By that time, a dazed PK wandered through the dining room doorway and made his way to Aaron who rubbed the cat's neck. PK settled down underneath the table.

I could tell Effie was staring at Yancy and the reason was obvious. The bruises we noticed yesterday were turning a yellowish-purple today.

Effie looked toward Yancy and said, "How did you get the bruises on your face? Did Romeo beat you?"

Yancy flinched. "I don't think he used a closed fist, but an open hand slap can be about as painful."

Falcon turned to Yancy. "You told us you remembered a sharp pain when he grabbed you."

"Yeah. I figured it was a stun gun," she said.

Falcon continued, "That could knock you out for a few seconds, but for him to transport you five blocks to where he held you would take more. What do you remember about waking up?"

Yancy leaned back and closed her eyes. When she reopened them, she said, "I recall a sweet smell."

"Chloroform," Falcon said. "It would keep you under plenty long enough for him to move you to his prison. What else can you think of that might help us?"

Yancy repeated her meditation process. "There was something strange about his speech pattern. As a reporter, I tune my ear to the way people talk. He doesn't use contractions."

We all remained quiet for a moment. I think we were all picturing speech patterns without a contraction.

Leaning forward, Yancy said, "I've never met anyone who doesn't slip an occasional contraction into their speech. It just isn't normal."

"Fits his pattern," Falcon said. "Romeo is anything but normal. Can anyone think of a reason a person would speak that way?"

We looked at one another, but no one spoke. I kicked things off. "Maybe he was subject to an extreme formal education."

"I wonder if it was his upbringing rather than education," Aaron said.

"I once took an English class from a teacher who enforced peculiar rules," Effie said. "She didn't use contractions very often and even pronounced the 'g' on the end of 'ing' words, sorta like 'ingah.' She tried to force the whole class to do the same, but for the most part, it didn't take."

Becca said, "I'd vote for a strict parent. I don't think a teacher would have the time and capability to beat that habit into a kid."

The doorbell rang. I said, "After this day, I don't suppose it can get any weirder." Looking through the peephole in the front door, I added, "I was wrong."

51

I OPENED MY FRONT DOOR AND INVITED GENE MORSE into the living room. He stood there dressed in casual slacks and shirt with green surgical booties on his feet. The rest of our group crowded out of the dining room and gawked.

Pointing to Gene's feet, I said, "What are you doing here dressed like that?"

He put a hand to his throat and handed me a note. All I saw was the word "laryngitis" before Falcon snatched the paper away from me.

He muscled Gene against the wall and patted him down. "Don't move until I've read all of this."

Gene looked over his shoulder at me. The expression said: what did I do?

I told everybody about Gene; how he shoved me out of the way of a falling body last fall and that we ran into each other at the mall and ate lunch together a couple of times.

Falcon finished the note and told Gene he could turn around and relax, then related the contents of the note to us. It mirrored the story Kenley Longstreet told us—down to the green booties. "Do you still have the instructions?" Falcon said to Gene.

Gene shook his head.

"Did the instructions tell you to destroy it?"

He nodded.

"By the way, what's your full name?" Falcon said.

He motioned like he was writing on a pad. Falcon said, "No. Surely you can at least say your name."

"Eugene Wayne Morse." The words sounded like they came from the throat of a frog.

Falcon stared at him and said, "Someone is playing a joke on you Mr. Morse. There's no sense hanging around here." Handing him a business card, Falcon said, "If you hear anything further, give me a call."

Gene Morse shrugged his shoulders and turned toward the door. As he reached for the knob, his sleeve slid up a few inches. I noticed the skin on the back of his wrist was shiny; like a healed scar. I frowned and dismissed it. I watched the group move back into the dining room, then opened the front door and Gene walked toward the elevator. I closed the door and watched through the peephole until the elevator doors slid closed behind Gene. When I turned, Falcon was on his cell phone and I heard him direct Benton to run a background check on Morse.

The group regathered at the dining room table and everyone was clamoring for me to tell them more about Gene. "I told you almost everything I know. He asked me out on a date, but I was more interested in Dennis Epstein at the time."

"And, how about now?" Becca said.

"I'd still like to date Dennis, but our schedules have been out of sync for weeks," I said.

Becca waggled a finger at me. "No. I was asking about Gene."

"Oh. No real desire there. I ate lunch with him to get out of a dinner date. I think we ran into each other twice in the past month or so." I looked at Falcon. "What all was in the note he brought?"

"I left it on the table by the front door. Let me get it." He returned in a few seconds. "It's not there. Did anyone pick it up?" Head shakes all around the table. "Damn. Morse must have taken it on his way out. I'm getting too old for this business."

I said, "You gotta remember what was in it."

"I scanned it. I didn't memorize it," Falcon said. "It was the same story Longstreet told us: instruction note, destroy it, gave this address, wear surgical booties since it's a crime scene, couldn't talk because he was suffering from laryngitis."

"If his note told you about destroying the instructions, why did you ask him about that?" Effie said.

"I was testing him to see if he would forget and try to speak."

Yancy's notepad was in her hand and she pointed with the pen in the other hand. "Was there anything unusual about the words—or his phrasing in the note?"

Falcon stared hard at her. "No, nothing I can recall…and don't forget…you can't print anything until we arrest Romeo."

Yancy slipped the pen and pad back into her purse.

Effie said, "Did you notice, I think Mr. Morse was wearing a wig. Casey, you told us you thought Romeo was bald."

"Yes, I did. In case no one caught it, Kenley wears a rug as well." Trying to narrow down who Romeo might be was still confusing. Most of the group expressed an opinion about his identity, but nothing definitive emerged.

When the discussion died down, Falcon said, "It could be either Morse or Longstreet…or neither. Perhaps we'll know more when Benton gets back to us with the report on Mr. Morse."

I gave Falcon a spare key to my front door and we all headed for bed. Effie offered to let Yancy share her room and Becca would bunk with me. Falcon volunteered to wait in the living room until Benton returned. I drifted off to sleep a few minutes after my head hit the pillow. Sometime later, I heard voices from the living room. Figuring it was Benton and Falcon changing shifts, I started to get up; I wanted to see the background check on Gene Morse, but the strain of the past few days overtook me.

52

ROMEO WRAPPED HIS ARMS AROUND HIMSELF AND stretched to ease the cramps and tense muscles. He reached this vantage point early yesterday evening in time to watch three cars arrive at Casey's parking garage. He knew two of them were the same ones parked at that house in south Little Rock. The third vehicle, a maroon Celica, was unfamiliar, but he recognized Falcon as the driver and saw Rebecca Rider and Casey in the backseat.

He maintained his vigil. Forrest Benton left in a few minutes and returned at midnight. Falcon left around twelve-thirty—and all was quiet in the garage.

Now the morning light was penetrating the underground parking area from the entry ramp. Romeo's plan was firm in his mind. The only kink would be if the man Falcon was working with returned before Casey left for work. He wasn't positive she would go to work, but after taking so many days off, Romeo was sure her conscience would get the better of her. If she came down with one or two others, he could handle all of them with the Taser. If there were more—he caressed the pistol in his jacket pocket—he would have to shoot them. He pulled on his ski mask over the clear plastic mask which also disguised him and moved into a position between two cars parked next to Casey's Mustang.

53

THE LIGHT STREAMED IN MY BEDROOM WINDOW the next time I rolled over in bed. I remembered wanting to get up last night to see the report Benton brought, but the stress got the best of me. By the time I reached the kitchen, everyone except Becca was there sipping coffee.

Effie bustled around taking breakfast orders and sliding plates of ham and eggs onto the table. I sat down and Benton shoved a sheaf of papers toward me. "There's not a whole lot of info in it," he said. "I can trace him back about six years. Before then, it's as if he didn't exist. Reports self-employment income as an accountant, but the data is sparse."

"I need to go to work today," I said. "I told my boss I'd need a few days off, but I think I'm at my limit."

Benton protested, but I insisted. We settled on a compromise—he and Becca would go with me and he contacted Falcon to bring him up to date on the day's schedule. I browsed through Gene's background but found nothing beyond what Benton related to us.

Yancy packed up and was the first to leave. Aaron wasn't scheduled to fly today so he would stay home and Effie didn't need to leave for another hour. I loaded my handbag with the built-in holster. The three of us gathered at my front door. Benton led the way down the elevator to the parking garage. We were nearing my car when Becca remembered her overnight bag. I tossed her my door key and she headed back upstairs.

I reached my car and Benton was telling me he would follow in his Toyota. A figure popped up behind Benton and stuck something against his neck. The sizzling sound was familiar and I thought of the day Romeo kidnapped me. "Damn," I said. "Not again."

Benton slumped to the concrete and the figure pointed the Taser at me. A familiar voice said, "Yes, again. Come with me or you will get zapped as well." He jerked me along and shoved me through the driver's door of a compact silver SUV. He slid in and pushed me down onto the floor on the passenger side. As he gunned the vehicle out of the parking spot, I heard a voice yelling. I rose up and saw Becca racing toward us before Romeo shoved me down again.

I fished my cell phone out of my pocket and turned it on. Romeo hit the brakes and I knew we were approaching the ninety-degree turn onto the exit ramp. I did a déjà vu of my previous escape. I hoped with all my might I wouldn't dislocate a shoulder again—or worse.

I hit the cement and rolled. I was luckier than last time and could hear Becca screaming at Benton for the keys to the Celica. Before I could get to my feet, the maroon Toyota roared out of its parking spot and screeched to a stop next to me. Becca leaned across the front seat, pushed the right door open and shouted for me to get in.

I scrambled into the coupe and the acceleration slammed the door shut. Becca said, "Buckle up, girl. It's gonna be a wild ride."

Becca seemed as much at home behind the wheel of this high-powered Celica as she did in her Firebird. She left the side street, swung left and slid into a small gap in the eastbound traffic. Playing the gas pedal and transmission, she weaved in and out, gaining on the line of cars heading downtown. We shot along Chenal Parkway, but when it became Financial Centre, a dead-stop jam loomed ahead of us. She cut left to the opposite side of the median. We were lucky the westbound lanes were almost empty. A heavy horn warned several out of our way and she slammed to a stop at the Shackleford Road red light.

I could see our silver quarry a half-mile ahead accelerating on I-630 toward town. "If we don't get through this red light," I said, "he'll be gone."

The traffic signal began its red-green cycle to a different direction. One set of cars stopped and before the opposite direction could start, Becca zipped through the red light and the chase was on again. Romeo was still visible three-quarters of a mile ahead. "Have you got a cell phone?" I said.

"Where's yours?"

"I stuck it under Romeo's front seat."

Becca struggled to free her phone from her slacks' pocket and handed it to me. I dialed Dennis first but got his voice mail and hung up. Falcon answered on the first ring. "Listen carefully," I said. "We're kinda busy right now. Call Dennis and brief him. We're eastbound on I-630 on Romeo's tail." I looked at the speedometer needle bouncing around the ninety mark. "Oh, my God."

"What's going on?" Falcon shouted.

"We're gaining on Romeo—he's in a silver Honda CR-V. He grabbed me, but I escaped. Before I jumped out of his truck, I turned my cell phone on and left it under his front seat. See if Dennis can trace the signal. I'll do my best to keep you posted, but at this speed I can barely hang on."

I heard Falcon start to say something and the phone went silent. I stared at it and the battery signal told the story—flatter than a mashed armadillo.

"Battery's dead," I said.

"I hope Falcon got all that. We're gonna need help soon."

There was a brief respite between packs of cars and Becca said, "You still got an eyeball on him?"

"Yeah. Tail end of that next batch of cars. In the far-right lane." I could see the University Avenue interchange coming up and Romeo pulled onto the shoulder and shot past a couple of cars trying to exit. "We're gaining," I said.

Becca downshifted and clipped the back bumper of a midsize sedan as she emulated Romeo's move. "I think he's going for an exit," she said.

Romeo took the off-ramp for Fair Park Boulevard. When we hit the ramp, he was nowhere in sight.

"Which way?" Becca yelled as she braked hard for the red traffic light ahead. "North or south?"

"Go north, left. It winds near Ray Winder Field and he stashed a get-away car there once before."

"Okay. Is it clear on the right?"

"Clear," I shouted. She dropped the transmission into second and the red light overhead was a blur as she made the corner.

We rounded a bend in the road and he was nine to ten car lengths ahead of us. It must have been obvious to him his acceleration was no match for ours, and he began zigzagging through the streets in an effort to lose us. Becca did a four-wheel drift around a tight right-hander and this time he was nowhere in sight. There was a strip mall on each side of the street and Becca slowed. We rubbernecked looking for the truck. Nothing. "He has to be here," I said. "There wasn't enough time to make that next corner."

Becca nodded. She cruised the mall parking lot on the left. Again nothing. At the end of the building, she turned and we moved down the delivery lane behind the mall building. When we reached the end, she said, "Crap. Let's check the one across the street."

We repeated our search pattern. Behind this one we found each unit was served by a steel, roll-up door large enough to accommodate delivery vehicles. It was my turn for an expletive. Becca pulled to a stop in the front parking lane.

"No way he got away from us," she said. "He has to be in one of the stores in this mall. This one has a place to stash his truck. The one over there…" She waved toward the mall across the street, "doesn't. I say he's got to be here."

Parking rows paralleled the mall and she pulled into the second row away from the building. "No sense being an obvious target if he's in there," Becca said. The car moved at a snail's pace while we looked at each of the businesses. At the end of the aisle, she stopped and we looked at each other shaking our heads. She said, "Let's make another pass."

Becca completed a U-turn and we cruised along the reverse path. The Celica was idling along in first gear and we checked each mall unit. About two-thirds of the way down the row, Becca stomped the clutch and brake and we did a head-snapping stop.

"What?" I said.

"Gimme a minute."

She was looking past me toward the building. I could see her eyes dart back and forth, her pointing finger moving in an odd pattern. Now she was looking down in her lap.

"What?"

Becca's head came up in a slow deliberate manner and her arm shot out past my nose. She seemed to be pointing at the fourth business from the end of the building, and she said, "That's the one. Romeo's in there."

54

BECCA'S POINTING FINGER WAS STILL IN FRONT OF my nose. I said, "You mean that do-it-yourself pottery shop?"

"Yep."

"What in the world makes you say that?"

"Look at the name—Semore Ceramics. It's an anagram for Morse's first initial and last name."

I stared at the storefront. "There's no 'G' in that name."

"I know. But his first name is Eugene, not Gene. Hey, I just thought of something else…'member how all the messages on the cards ended?"

I said, "Yes, there were two dashes, so what?"

"In Morse code—how's that for a tie-in—two dashes stand for the letter M, you know for Romeo's last name."

If she was correct, this meant Becca not only solved an anagram puzzle, but also identified the fact that Romeo was Gene Morse. I looked at the dead cell phone and wished we could pass this information on to Dennis and Falcon. My head swiveled and my eyes took in the parking lot. I didn't see any pay phones. "Two choices," I said. "We can look for a phone or we can confront the bastard."

"I vote for the second choice. His plans don't seem to be working out and he may be destroying evidence or packing up to make his escape. You've got your gun, don't you?"

My bag with the built-in holster was still slung over my shoulder. "Yes. I almost forgot I was carrying it." I eased the Glock from its nest, racked the slide and placed it back in the holster.

Becca reversed until she located a parking spot and backed into the space. I angled through the parked cars away from the ceramics store. "We'll hit the sidewalk far enough down, no one in the shop will see us coming," I said.

"What's our plan when we get to his shop?" she said.

We stopped when we reached the sidewalk and discussed our strategy. After several minutes our plan consisted of: go through the front door and confront Romeo. Not sophisticated, but simple.

The door to the shop was on the side of the storefront nearest to us as we approached. We didn't have a chance to see who might be inside before we hit the entrance. I reached for the handle, pushed it open and we entered almost side-by-side. We stopped short. A tall bald man was standing behind a counter that was large enough to hold a cash register and little more. The place was full of small tables and shelves on two walls holding pottery in various stages of completion. Becca looked at me. I looked at Becca and her expression mirrored my thoughts: who the hell is this guy?

My mind worked at incredible speed, and I stammered out, "Me and my friend want to make some pottery."

He smiled and said, "You've come to the right place." We chatted about ceramics. Rather, he talked ceramics and we nodded our heads. "Since you're new to the hobby we have a start-up plan. For twenty dollars each, you get three lessons and make whatever type piece you'd like."

I gave him a pair of twenties. He rang up the sale and held out a receipt. Handing us each an apron, he pointed to some doors. "You can change in there."

Becca and I entered separate rooms. That was a misnomer. The cubicle wasn't big enough to turn around in. I wondered why we needed to change when we could have slipped the apron over our heads. I held my arms close to my sides and managed to do a one-eighty. Draping the apron loop over my head, I reached for the door handle. It wouldn't turn. I thought it must be stuck, so I twisted harder and pulled with all my strength. I noticed a sweet smell in the air and the room went black.

55

WHEN I AWOKE, THE SWEET SMELL WAS STILL THERE and my head throbbed. I slumped in whatever I was tied to. My chin rested on my chest, and I eased one eye half open. All I could see was a pair of legs tied at the ankles with Duct Tape—the shoes belonged to Becca. Closing the first eye, I opened the other one a bit. Another pair of shoes greeted me. I was almost positive these were the same ones Gene Morse wore under the green booties at my place yesterday. It looked like the same clothes he wore then as well. I decided to play unconscious, closed the eye and waited for someone else to make the first move.

After what seemed to be an eternity, I heard something stirring and eased the first eye open again. Becca's feet were moving. Figuring Gene's attention would be on her, I shifted my gaze. His feet were turned away from me, so I lifted my head, opening the eye all the way. Same clothes, but this was a bald man wearing a plastic mask over his face. I was able to survey the room. The contents included shelves, benches and tables that indicated we were in the back area of the pottery store. A large silver object sat near one wall and I assumed it was a ceramics firing kiln. On the wall above the kiln was a sign which read: No ceramics firing on Thursdays—kiln is cooled down and cleaned on Friday. Near it sat a foot-powered potter's wheel.

My attention was pulled back to Becca; she was making a low moaning sound. The man leaned down toward her and whispered something in her ear. His voice was too low for me to make out the words. Without turning, he said in a loud voice,

"No sense pretending any longer, Casey. I know you are not still unconscious."

"What should I call you?"

Even behind the plastic mask, I could see his lips curl upward in a smile. He hooked a thumb under the chin of the face covering and pulled it off. "You can call me Romeo or Gene. Your choice."

"Who's your sidekick out front?" I said.

"He runs the shop when I am not around. He has no knowledge of Romeo's activities."

Becca moaned. We both looked at her in time to see her head come up. The expression on her face told me we were sharing the same headache. She struggled against the Duct Tape and said, "What the hell is going on?"

Gene leaned down toward her. "All in good time, dear lady. All in good time."

"In case you missed it, Gene let me know he is Romeo," I said to Becca.

She looked at him. "Mystery solved. I guess we can all go home now."

Gene threw his head back and roared with laughter. When his sides stopped heaving, he said, "I love a good sense of humor, however I fear that neither of you will be going home."

His words sent a chill down my spine, and I wondered how we could keep him occupied until the cavalry arrived. I was banking on the chance Falcon heard all my last words on the phone and that Dennis could track the signal from my cell, which was still in Romeo's truck. My resolve was fading and I experienced a flashback to a time when Jarvis, my ex, berated me for some decision of mine he decided was stupid. That day, I fell apart and hid in our bedroom for hours crying until I could no longer hold my eyes open. I was having that same feeling— sinking into that same black abyss. I forced that vision out of my mind. Get your ass in gear, Casey, and figure out how to get the best of this asshole.

Becca beat me to it. She began asking Gene questions about the ceramics shop, the car chases and the murders. He didn't seem concerned about time and responded to all her queries. My eyes moved around the room, looking for a way out. The area we were in was not as wide as the storefront. I figured the door in one side wall led to a garage served by the steel roll-up door. There should be plenty of room to hide his vehicle. My purse was lying on a table against the opposite wall at least thirty feet away. The only other door was one that must have led to the alleyway behind the mall building.

I heard Becca ask about the man out front. "Oh, he has gone home," Gene said. "As soon as you two were asleep in the booths, I sent him out. The store is closed for the day."

Another icy feeling shot along my back. When he took off his mask, he removed the last vestige of disguise. I knew, and I was sure Becca was aware, his decision was made—we would both have to die.

56

GENE TURNED HIS ATTENTION BACK TO ME. "IT IS time I get to my plans for you. I do not know how much time we have left before an interloper appears." He moved toward the oven and peered at a gauge that looked like a thermometer. He returned and said, "Not too long now before my kiln reaches maximum heat."

"What happens then?" I said.

"I will be able to dispose of any evidence I have in here."

He smiled and I shivered. The oven was too small to hold a whole person, but I wondered about body parts. I gave Becca a look, doing my best to convey the question: Do you have any ideas? She gave me a wide-eyed look and shook her head. Either she didn't have a shred of an idea, or more likely she had no idea what my grimace meant.

Now it was my turn to buy time. My mind seemed devoid of thought. One lonesome idea did ricochet around inside my skull…minor problem, it would not come into focus. Fearing I would lose the opportunity all together, I opened my mouth to see what would emerge. "So you think you've left no tracks at all?"

His expression belied his confidence and I pressed ahead. "Yep, I bet you think you did away with all the evidence." The word "fingerprint" came clear to my thought process.

Gene glared at me. "I left every crime scene sterile—barren of anything which could identify me."

"I'm sure you believe that, but you are wrong." I started to mention the partial print on the blank postcard, but thought better of it. The longer he was in the dark about details, the more of his time I could waste.

"What possible evidence could there be? You see that kiln over there?" He waved an arm toward the oven and didn't wait for me to reply. "I always wore more than one layer of clothing, so I would not leave any personal traces behind. When I returned afterwards, I disposed of all my clothing and footwear. My faithful kiln reduces everything to a fine ash."

I was afraid he was winding down. Time to prod him again. "How about someone going through the ashes?"

"That would do no good." He threw both arms out in an expansive gesture like an actor taking a curtain call. "I use a powerful little vacuum cleaner to remove the ash. It, as well as the contents, are scattered across the countryside. No, my dear Casey, I do not believe I have left anything behind in the way of clues or evidence."

As he was talking, I did my best to sneak a look at my watch. Between Becca and my questions, he had been talking for nearly a half hour.

Gene was silent and when my gaze returned to him he said, "You are not banking on Falcon or your police friend to show up, are you?"

"How in the world would they know where we are?"

"How indeed?" he said.

Gene smiled at me. I can't describe it, but that same chill was tap dancing up and down my vertebra. He reached into a pocket and produced a cell phone and with another of those expansive gestures, he flipped it open and said, "Recognize this, Casey?"

It was my cell phone, and it was turned off. Then he opened his other hand and showed me the battery from my phone—there was no rescue effort riding my beam from a cell tower.

57

I COULD SEE BECCA'S EYES SCANNING AROUND THE room. I'm sure she also recognized our dilemma and was look-ing for a way out. Since my consciousness came back, I worked at the tape on my wrists, but it was not loose enough to make any difference. The tape end was pulled up from the rest, but I couldn't find a way to unwrap it from my wrists. It was a five-sec-ond dash to the table where my purse rested…assuming I could get my hands free in that amount of time.

I also didn't know whether Gene was carrying a gun or could get to one hidden in the shop. Whatever we were going to do would be up to the two of us. I held no illusions of a rescuer charging through a door.

Gene was moving around the room behind me. I whispered to Becca, "What's he up to?"

"Keeps adding papers from a file drawer to a stack on a table back there. He's damn picky about which ones he adds to the pile."

"Shut up over there," he said.

I heard footsteps approach though I still couldn't see him. The sound stopped and something smacked into the back of my head.

If snakes could speak, they would sound like him. "Doing a bit of plotting, are we?" He stepped around my chair so we could both see him and said, "Some documents, more than others, might shed light on me. I want to be certain they do not survive the fire that destroys my little shop here." He pivoted on one foot to return to his work behind me.

"That won't get rid of the other evidence we have," I said as I twisted my head around far enough to see him. That struck a nerve. Gene did his best to cover, but I saw the slight stutter-step as he turned around. He continued toward the area behind me. I could hear him rustling papers when he said, "What other evidence? I did not leave anything behind."

I said, "What makes you think you are so clean?" I hoped he would rise to the bait. He did.

Gene stood beside my chair and began to cover the details of his deeds and what he did to cover his tracks—from the first card and killing to the final blank postcard. This time he didn't catch me looking at my watch. Between his diatribe and my questions egging him on, another forty minutes were behind us.

He leaned down. "You have not even touched on the most important aspect." He paused. "Why you, Casey? Why you?"

He was right. In all our deliberations and discussions, none of us figured out the "why me" facet. "Okay," I said. "Why did you pick me?" With luck, this ought to be good for another fifteen to twenty minutes of diatribe from him.

"It was not a random pick. Oh, I suppose you could call it a coincidence the way I met you. I was arriving at the TrueTemp Agency to interview for a job as you were leaving. I decided to learn more about you. I followed you home and to your job interview the following morning. It was no accident I was there when the body fell at the Midtown Atrium Towers Building."

My God. He's been stalking me since last fall. "You mean to tell me you picked me out of the entire population of Little Rock because of a chance meeting."

"Yes, my dear. I suppose you could call it a chance meeting."

"Then why did you wait so long to start sending postcards?" And killing people.

The gasp came from Becca. "You mean Gene here has been after you all this time? Why the hell you doing all this, you nut job?"

Her comment brought him up short, but I wondered if it was the best tact under the circumstances. The look on Gene's face told me it wasn't.

"You best keep your smart mouth shut. I plan to make your demise as painless as possible, but with comments like those, I may change my mind."

"Oh, piss off, shit head," Becca said.

I cringed. When Gene turned his back on us, I saw a slight smile on her face. She was baiting him. It might work. If he got agitated enough, he might make a mistake and give us a chance.

Gene reduced a foot-high stack of papers to ash in the kiln. I assumed they were ashes because earlier he bragged his little evidence-reducer ran hotter than a cremation oven.

"How long does it take for that thing to cool down?" I said. He didn't respond, but I figured we were safe for a couple of hours or so. Of course, he could kill us while waiting for the damn thing to cool enough to vacuum it out. Not a comforting thought.

There was a banging sound out in the front area of the shop. Someone was beating on the front door. Gene stopped, listened, put an index finger to his lips and waited…and waited. The banging continued. With a curse on his lips, he stormed through the door to the shop area.

58

BECCA AND I BOTH STOOD, WHICH WAS AWKWARD
since our ankles were still bound with tape. I hopped over to her
and turned around. "The end of the tape on my wrists is pulled
loose—can you get it off?" I could feel her fingers fumbling
over my hands and wrists. Grunting, groaning, muttering and
cursing came from behind me. Fingers got purchase on the tape
end and she tugged and pulled. I could tell she unwrapped the
first layer and I twisted my hands.

"Shit," she said. "Hold still until I can get more of it loose."

The next layer was gone and I felt my wrists parting. I
stopped and cocked an ear toward the front shop. The voice
sounded like Yancy's. She was talking far too loud to be carrying on a normal conversation and I couldn't hear Gene's
side of the discussion. "It's Yancy out there. She's doing her
best to let us know she's here," I said. My ankles were free
of the tape now and I hobbled toward the workbench where
my handbag lay.

"You cannot go back there," Gene shouted.

Yancy said, "Who the hell says I can't?"

"I do," was Gene's reply and then we heard a shot.

"Damn," Becca said. "Hope he didn't kill her. I like that gal."
By this time, she was free of tape as well and made her way to the
opposite wall full of shelves holding unfired pottery. "Someone's
gonna be pissed," she said. "When he comes through the door,
I'm going to bombard him with these." She was brandishing
three pots in one hand, and I was trying to figure out how she
was holding them all.

I pulled the Glock from its holster and gathered the spare magazine. Scrambling to a spot near the wall and behind the kiln, I dumped over a workbench. Not much cover, but better than nothing. Gene crashed through the door shoving Yancy along in front of him. She didn't appear wounded, so I assumed the shot was to warn her off. A clay pot smashed into the wall near Gene's head and Yancy wrenched free. "Yancy, get down," I said loud enough to carry the distance to her. She did and I fired a round at Gene. Two more pottery missiles hit the wall and Gene flinched. I saw Becca grab for several more pieces. So far, she was doing a better job than me when it came to pinning him down. Yancy crab-crawled toward the spot where Becca was hunkered down behind an overturned worktable.

By the time I aimed at Gene again, he was peering over the sights of a large, semi-auto pistol. Before I could squeeze off a shot, he let three fly at me. Two hit the wall above my head and the third one pinged off the metal skin of the oven. Without aiming, I shoved my gun around the side of the kiln and pulled the trigger twice hoping I could at least drive him back through the door. It didn't work.

More clay pots flew hitting Gene and the wall behind him. The fusillade was too much for one person, so I figured Yancy was joining Becca in the pottery brigade. He dove for cover, overturning a table as he went, and I took the opportunity to drag my table closer. Between the metal oven and the table, I had darn good concealment. His head popped up and he fired three more times. Best I could tell, one hit the table I was behind. The other two must have gone wide. I peeked around the end of my barricade and saw him fire twice in Becca and Yancy's direction. I was glad Gene furnished his store with sturdy wood furniture. The tabletops seemed to be absorbing the rounds fired. Fine for the home team, but it afforded him the same cover.

Gene fired four more times. I think he aimed two at me and the others toward my cohorts. I took a breath to assess the situation. If I counted correctly, Gene fired his weapon thirteen times and I still had seven of the ten rounds I started with. The extra magazine in my pocket held an additional ten cartridges. No telling how many he had left. He could have reloaded or be using oversize magazines or both. Which way out? The back door was a good twenty feet away from me and no doubt locked. Could I blow the lock apart from this distance? Which way would Gene try to go? The door to the front shop was closest. The garage door where his SUV must be parked would force him to pass between our two locations; the back door was the farthest sprint for him.

I guessed Gene would go for his vehicle and if he did, we could block the door to the garage behind him and go for our own car. "Yancy? Do you have a cell phone?" I called out. When she gave a positive response, I said, "Call Dennis and Falcon. We need help bad."

"You got it," she said.

I was watching as she eased her head around the end of her table where Gene couldn't see her. She pointed to her phone, shook her head and gave me a thumbs-down gesture. Damn, how many more dead phones do we have to suffer? She was smart enough to let me know, without giving up the fact to Gene, that we had no way of communicating with the outside world.

I fired a round over the top of the table in Gene's direction without aiming. No chance of hitting him, but I could remind him I was still a player. Three shots pinged off the metal kiln— Gene was letting me know he was still in the game too.

59

WITHOUT RAISING MY HEAD ABOVE MY PROTECTIVE barricade, I shouted, "Gene, I'm surprised you're no longer interested in the evidence you left behind."

His voice came from the same spot as the previous shots. "I do not believe you. I think you are doing your best to confuse me and waste time…and it is not working."

"You're wrong, Gene. We have your fingerprint and it would only have been a matter of time before we closed in on you."

He didn't respond, and I could almost see the wheels in his head turning.

Yancy chimed in. "Bet you'd like to know how I found you as well."

Becca said, "Yeah, girl. How the hell did you find us?"

"We've got a super-techie at the newspaper," Yancy said. "I had him run some names: Kenley Longstreet, Gene Morse; even Casey's ex-husband, looking for a connection. The only name we could trace anything to was Morse. He owned this business which seemed to be suspicious and under the radar."

Morse remained silent. I eased my head around the end of the table trying to get a glimpse of him. I drew my head back and there was a loud thud as another worktable was upended. I took one more look and saw what he was doing. The second table gave him further cover and he could move closer to us. Another shot and wood splinters hit my face. Gene was getting smarter. I think he used the sound of the table hitting the floor as a diversion. When I rose to the bait, he loosed a well-aimed shot from behind the table and he damned near hit me in the head. Don't be that dumb again, Casey.

Thunk. Another table hit the floor. A quick peek from the other end of my table showed me about twenty feet of cover he could use. The direction of his concealment was aimed at the position where Yancy and Becca were exposed.

Thunk. Another table going over and then I heard a pottery barrage hit the wall near Gene. Becca was yelling, "Cover fire."

I rose and saw Gene aim at my two cohorts as they scrabbled for their new shelter. He fired once and I loosed three rounds at him. I thought I saw him wince before he dove behind his tables. "Are you okay?" I shouted to the two.

"That son-of-a-bitch shot me," Becca yelled back.

"How bad is it?" I said.

Yancy responded. "It's in the leg, and I don't think it's too bad…looks like a through and through. Keep the bastard away from us while I patch Becca up."

I looked at the Glock. One in the chamber and two left in this mag. I popped the magazine out, shoved the fresh one in and pocketed the first one. I rose again, let go with three more rounds and waited for a response. None. No sign of Gene. "How's it going, Yancy?"

"I've got the bleeding pretty well stopped—don't think it hit an artery or anything—but she needs to see a doctor."

I was scanning the three overturned tables and still didn't see Gene anywhere. I gave myself a mental smack on the forehead for not noticing the door before. "I think the son-of-a-bitch's going out the front," I yelled over my shoulder. "Toss me the keys to the Celica." There was a jingle of keys hitting the floor behind me. I snatched them up and stood.

Keeping my gun up in a two-handed grip, I advanced toward the door to the shop's front area. I peered into the storefront and there was still no sign of Gene.

The sound of a steel roll-up door caught my attention.

"I think he's going for his truck from the outside," Becca shouted from the backroom.

"Yancy, get Becca to a hospital. I'm going after him." I was out the front door before she could answer.

60

GENE MORSE DUCKED UNDER THE STEEL DOOR AS IT rolled upward, nursing his right arm as he hurried to the SUV. He rested against the driver's door for a moment. The run from the front of his ceramics shop to the roll-up exit at the rear of the mall building winded him. Hauling himself in behind the wheel, he cursed when he reached for the ignition.

"Damn that woman. After all I planned to do for her, Casey shot me." He swiped his right arm across his eyes to sweep the tears from his face and winced from the pain. Gene wrapped a rag he found on the floor of the vehicle around his upper arm. The damage appeared superficial and he could bandage it later. With the truck in gear, he wheeled out of the garage happy with his foresight. "Backing into the garage was an intelligent move."

Steering with one arm proved more of a problem than he anticipated. Gene banged the side of the SUV against the door-jamb as he exited the garage. He whipped the wheel straight and accelerated down the alleyway behind the building.

"Damn. This is the one day there is traffic back here." He stared at the maroon Toyota hurtling toward him.

61

I RACED ACROSS THE MALL'S PARKING LOT TOWARD the Toyota Becca parked earlier. Inside the car, I hesitated for a second, wondering which direction Gene would take. Turning right, I veered into the lane between rows of parked cars, cleared the last one and took a hard left. I raced past the end of the mall building and cranked the wheel left, steering into the lane behind the building.

A silver Honda SUV was approaching head-on. "I got here before you could get away, you bastard," I said to an empty car. I wonder how good he was at playing chicken. I gulped and wondered how good I was.

The distance narrowed between the two vehicles. Five car lengths. Four car lengths…three…two. I cut the wheel to the right as Gene did the same—he crunched his right front fender on a steel door and the Celica scraped the concrete block wall on my right. Not enough room to turn around here. Maybe I can beat him to the street out front. He disappeared around the far end of the building in my rearview mirror just before I swung around the opposite end. Arriving at the street entrance of the parking lot, I screeched to a stop. Craning my neck, I was hoping for a glimpse of the silver SUV. "Hot damn. The fates are with me," I said and accelerated into the street hot on Gene's back bumper.

He turned into a side street and we were southbound on Van Buren and then on Fair Park. "This is almost the reverse of the exact course he took to his shop. I bet he's headed for I-630 again." My assumptions were right and now he was on the expressway doing eighty and I was about a dozen feet behind him. He braked hard to make the left-handed curve bending toward I-30 northbound. I glued the Celica to his back bumper.

Once on the interstate, he swerved hard to the left and was running in the center breakdown lane, which wasn't really a lane. He was squeezing by what little traffic there was by blasting his horn. I could see the bridge over the Arkansas River coming up fast.

Traffic was thin and I tried to come up on his right side, hoping to force him into the concrete barrier separating us from southbound cars. He must have seen me coming because he cut the wheel hard right. His SUV shot past in front of me and began to swerve.

Gene made two violent overcorrections, struck a compact car a glancing blow and the Honda tipped up on the right hand wheels. Struggling for balance, it teetered as it careened down the highway and then rolled over on its side. I saw him roll sideways at least three times before he struck the outside concrete retaining wall and bounce upward. The car pirouetted on its front bumper for an eternity.

62

GENE'S VEHICLE WAS POISED ON THE FRONT BUMPER until inertia and gravity gained the upper hand. The SUV flipped over the outside bridge railing and plunged toward the river below.

I moved into the right side breakdown lane and stopped a hundred feet past the point Gene's car went off the bridge. By the time I scrambled out of my Celica and peered over the side of the roadway, his car was out of sight in the swift current.

It took an hour's worth of high-speed talking before I convinced the police who arrived on the scene I was not the bad guy here, and they could better spend their time dragging the river for Gene's car. One of the uniformed officers, who arrived in the third or fourth car, remembered seeing me with Dennis at the Markham Road police station. A call to Dennis, on a borrowed phone, got me on the right track and I explained the details of the day including the fact Yancy would be taking Becca to a hospital. One of the officers nearby overheard the details and was making notes. The borrowed phone rang; he answered it and handed it back to me. It was Dennis again and he told me Becca was already at the hospital being treated in the emergency room. He asked me to join him there. The request was enough for the cops on the bridge to assign one of the cars and a driver to get me to the trauma center at University Hospital.

When I arrived at the ER, I found Becca had been treated and must be feeling fine. I heard her voice long before I was ushered to the curtained cubicle. Her bandaged leg was supported by a pillow and she was holding sway regaling the staff with her prowess with pottery. Her version barely acknowledged the fact that my Glock played any sort of role in the outcome. It was hard to fault her, so I put an arm around her and squeezed her in a hug.

"Hey there, girlfriend," Becca said. "Careful with the walking wounded."

Dennis took a call on his cell and returned to Becca's bedside. "This should wrap things up. Morse left enough prints in his ceramics shop we were able to match one to the print on the blank postcard. There's no doubt he was Romeo and there's little doubt he died in the river."

"What do you mean, little doubt he died?" I said.

"Salvagers who were working nearby were able to locate his car and hoist it out of the water. It was empty…but the river current is running high and the Coast Guard folks don't think he had a chance of surviving. If the fall didn't kill him, he surely drowned."

I looked around the room at my friends and felt comfortable. I would have preferred to have more finality to the demise of Gene Morse and Romeo, but decided I could live with this situation.

By this time, everyone on and hand and crowded into Becca's cubicle. I said, "I think we owe poor Kenley Longstreet an explanation and an apology for getting him involved in this mess."

Effie stepped forward and said, "Casey, we could have a buffet at your place. Aaron and I can put it together." She looked toward Aaron and said, "Is that okay with you?"

He nodded.

Dennis and Falcon looked ready to go. I took Becca's hand. "How about you? Feel up for a party?"

"You bet your bippy, girlfriend."

"Yancy, are you up for a champagne brunch?"

"As soon as I file my story with the paper this'll blow the socks off my editor," she said.

The charge nurse entered and gave Becca her discharge papers and a crutch. Everyone stood and marched toward the hospital exit. Well, all except Becca; she moved with a three-legged shuffle but was smiling all the way.

THE END

APPENDIX

Are you intrepid sleuths ready to join Casey's band? How many clues, did you identify?

- Romeo never used contractions; Gene Morse did likewise.

- In Romeo's story about killing his parents, he mentions burning his arm. At her condo, Casey notices a scar on his arm.

- Postcard messages ended with two dashes: —— which in Morse code is the letter M.

- Killing on Thursday—remember the sign on the wall by the kiln? Romeo cooled the kiln on Thursday after destroying evidence and cleaned it out on Friday.

- Each cryptic message is explained in the prose.

DECODING THE MESSAGE ON
THE FOURTH POSTCARD

Original coded message, listed in order

```
pznenp oziab7 bqlfdn 6qc4li 7qp24p
```

Message listed vertically in groups of 5, shown left to right

TABLE 1

p	z	n	e	n	p
o	z	i	a	b	7
b	q	l	f	d	n
6	q	c	4	l	i
7	q	p	2	4	p

Recopy Table 1; list each line, converting left to right characters into top to bottom columns

TABLE 2

p	o	b	6	7
z	z	q	q	q
n	i	l	c	d
e	a	f	4	2
n	b	d	l	4
p	7	n	i	p

Table 2 is listed in sequence, left
to right, top to bottom

```
pob67 zzqqq nilcp eaf42 nbdl4 p7nip
```

Simple substitution code is a reversed alphabet
(top is plain text, bottom is encoded).

```
abcdefghijklmnopqrstuvwxyz1234567890
ponmlkjihgfedcba0987654321zyxwvutsrq
```

Coded (top), decoded (bottom)

```
pob67zzqqqnilcdeaf42nbd14p7nip
about11000chenalpkwycomewatcha
```

Final "p" in code is a filler to make grids even

Message reads:

```
About 11000 Chenal Pkwy come watch
```

Romeo set up the message first, and then
worked backwards through the steps to
reach the coded message on the postcard.

ABOUT THE AUTHOR

John Achor's writing assignments have appeared in various local, national and international publications such as *Good Old Days, Computer Pilot, The Storyteller* and *Writers' Journal.* He enjoys writing about, "The subjects I know best: the military, flying and people I've known." After that, John says he lets a vivid imagination take over.

The first of his three careers spanned twenty years as a U.S. Air Force pilot. He accumulated over 4,000 hours flying planes from Piper Cubs to the military equivalent of the Boeing 707.

After the military, he entered the real estate industry. He joined a national real estate franchise as a management consultant working at the regional and national levels. Those positions led him to Phoenix, Arizona, and an affiliation with a major Savings & Loan institution.

In John's words, "When the Savings and Loan industry melted away like a lump of sugar in hot coffee, I knew it was time to develop a third career." He became a freelance computer instructor, user-developer, consultant, writer and Community College instructor.

In the 1990s, John began developing characters to fill ideas he had in mind for thrillers and mystery novels. The thriller series features Alex Hilliard, an Air Force pilot, and a thirty-something lady is the leading light in the Casey Fremont mystery series.

By the 2000s, he put five novels featuring Casey Fremont and Alex Hilliard in the can and launched his writing career. He and his wife left Arizona for Arkansas and later relocated to Nebraska. From there, John continues writing and has ideas in mind for a third thriller and has completed the first chapters of the fourth mystery novel.

WHAT'S COMING DOWN THE ROAD

In *Five, Six – Deadly Mix*, John Achor's amateur female detective, Casey Fremont, returns ready to tackle crime once more and along with her sidekicks become involved in another caper.

In this third Casey Fremont mystery, intrigue and real life drama collide for Casey in this exciting tale of deduction and death.

Casey Fremont lands in the middle of a combined local police/FBI investigation into fraud and theft at a local hospital. Also, two women have suspiciously fallen to their deaths before Casey reports for work in her undercover role.

Casey Fremont has a knack for solving mysteries…she also has a habit of flirting with danger—and this time it could well end with her death. Look for her "roomies" Effie Tremayne and Aaron Kincaid as well as Detective Sergeant Dennis Epstein and the enigmatic Falcon.

A short story by John Achor

MURDER IN D MAJOR AND D MINOR

(TWO SHARPS AND A FLAT)

Rhonda McQuaid's mind could only process only process one concept—I've got to get out of this town. Too many years doing the same dang thing—gotta get outta here.

Saturday night and she finished the second set at the Blue Rose, a smallish bar across the nearby county line from the only city for miles. The roadhouse owners chose this spot because the town was in a dry county and they could sell booze at this location. She eased her Les Paul Gibson electric guitar onto the vertical stand and stepped down from the stage. Elbowing past Sam Barstow, she moved to the small table reserved for performers. Reserved? Jammed into a dark corner, the table enjoyed no view of the stage and patrons and waitresses alike ignored it. The smell of stale beer and greasy fries did nothing to improve her disposition. I hate this town, she thought. I need to find a way to get to the Big City where I can be recognized for my talent.

Ted Carsten, the bartender, stood by the table as she arrived. He waited for her to take a seat before he put a paper napkin down on the table and placed a draft beer in front of her. "Rhonda, I'm sorry Sam is here tonight. Hope he's not going to hassle you."

"Sam can't get it through his thick head we're history. It's way over between us."

"Yeah, I know that. It's just…" Ted assumed his old hound dog–hang dog expression. "Well, if there's anything I can do for you…"

"You're a dear, Ted," Rhonda said. "I'll yell if I need help, and please ask Gretchen to put another bottle of water on the stage for me."

Rhonda was lost in thought when something blocked what little light reached the table. Looking up, she said, "Sam Barstow, there's nothing left for us to say. Please don't sit down or cause a scene."

Sam spoke in a low growling tone and animated his speech with arm gestures. She glanced toward the bar and saw Ted and his assistant, Gretchen, both watching. Ted said something to Gretchen, wheeled and walked away. Sam seemed exhausted and slumped into a chair.

Rhonda said, "It's almost time for my last set, Sam. Why don't you leave now?" She left him in the dark corner and returned to the stage.

Several minutes later, Sheriff Buster Richfield stepped onto the platform and interrupted the music. He spoke into the microphone. "Anyone know who the Ford F-150 with the fancy red and yellow paint job belongs to?" More than a few in the audience shouted the name. Buster cupped a hand behind one ear as if he couldn't hear or understand them.

Rhonda leaned over and said, "Sam. Sam Barstow owns that truck." The sheriff took Rhonda by the arm and produced handcuffs. "Well, ol' Sam's truck has a flat tire, and he's a layin' next to it a chewin' up gravel with a stab wound in his chest.

"What's that got to do with me?" Rhonda said.

"I heard him and you got into it here tonight. I think you mighta had something to do with his killin."

More than one person on the dance floor shouted an alibi for Rhonda saying she was on stage from before Sam walked out of the Blue Rose. Buster relented, let go of her arm and, in what he must have considered his most authoritative voice, said, "Don't leave town."

Rhonda and the group began to play again, but her heart wasn't in the music. At last, she stepped to the mike and said, "What the hell, folks. Let's call it a night." The crowd stopped dancing and nodded in unison. Rhonda slipped her guitar into the soft fabric case and returned it to its stand. She turned to see her, on again-off again boyfriend, Chet Longstreet grinning at her. He said, "C'mon, let's blow this joint."

"Oh, Chet. You always know how to sweet talk a gal." The sarcasm in her voice seemed lost on the hulking hunk in cowboy boots, western cut shirt and jeans. She liked him, but it was easy to see he was missing a lug nut or two in the culture department.

"Aw, damn, Rhonda. You know what I mean," he said.

On the way to the front door, Ted Carsten came out from behind the bar. "Sorry for all the trouble, Rhonda, Let me know if there's anything I can do to help."

"Keep your nose out of our business," Chet said. "We can make it just fine."

Rhonda jerked her arm from Chet's grip. "Don't be making decisions for the both of us. I can take care of my own world all by myself." Chet got his "hurt" look, stopped but said nothing. Rhonda continued out the door leaving him standing there with his mouth open.

In the parking lot, Rhonda looked past the sheriff and saw Sam Barstow still lying on his back in the gravel. Someone apparently rolled the body, because there was a large pool of blood next to him where his chest wound bled out. The truck was in the aisle leading out of the parking lot. She surmised Sam got into his truck without seeing the right rear tire was flat. Bet he was spraying gravel all over the place before he noticed the flat tire dragging on him. Must have got out to examine the tire when someone caught him there. Wonder if they snuck up on him or offered to help change the tire.

Rhonda walked toward her car and smiled at Sheriff Buster as she passed him. He repeated his earlier words, "Don't leave town." She smiled again and gunned out of the parking lot. In the rearview mirror, she saw Chet standing in the trail of dust and gravel billowing in her wake.

* * *

A week later, Rhonda was back on the bandstand at the Blue Rose. The picture of Sam Barstow lying on the parking lot gravel still filled her mind. Before tuning the guitar, she used her left thumb to check the calluses on the fingertips of her left hand. Having not practiced for the entire week, she was concerned the tips were getting soft and would be painful as she fingered the chords on her guitar.

Sheriff Buster strode close to the stage. He got Rhonda's attention and pointed to his eyes. Rhonda figured it was a signal telling her he was keeping an eye on her. Rather than acknowledge the gesture, she said "Buster, if you're trying to pick your nose, you missed." The sheriff turned and stalked to the bar.

The next time she looked up, Chet Longstreet was standing in front of the stage staring at her. He said, "Rhonda, how come you ain't paying me no mind this week?" Rhonda returned to the guitar tuning, so he continued, "C'mon, gal. Pay me some attention."

"I spent the week trying to figure out who killed Sam. I didn't have much time for dating."

"That's all well an' good," he said, "but I'm gettin' pretty horny sittin' around waitin' for you. If you don't start paying me more attention, I'm a gonna do something drastic about it."

"Don't be melodramatic, Chet." She looked over his shoulder and saw Ted standing a few feet behind him. Ted was holding a bottle of water and one foot was pawing the dance floor like a horse counting out the answer to a math problem. "Ted, come on up here with that water. Nobody's going to bite you."

Chet made a lunging motion toward him as if to attack but pulled up short. Ted flinched, then placed the water on the table. Chet stared at him the entire time, and Ted retreated to his place behind the bar.

The remaining members of the musical group assembled on the stage and began the evening's entertainment. The Four Studs & A Filly band billed themselves as a Country – Rock group. The leader handed out a song list, hand printed in pencil and copied so many times it was all but unreadable. Then he counted, one, two, one, two, three and they launched into the first set of the night.

Rhonda flailed at the steel strings of the Gibson without enthusiasm. She kept thinking back to last Saturday night and Sam's death. The fact Chet glared at her from his seat, never looking away, unnerved her. Near the end of the first set, Rhonda's pick flipped out of her fingers and disappeared behind the stage. She borrowed one from the other guitarist, but it wasn't the same as her own. At the intermission, she told the group she had spare picks in her car and would be back inside before they were due to take the stage again.

She walked toward the front door and noticed that Chet got up and was following her. Outside she wheeled and confronted him. "I don't need you traipsing after me." Her voice was louder than she expected.

It brought Chet up sharp. "Damnit, Rhonda. If you don't pay me more notice, I'll kick your butt from here to the county line."

"Considering it's only about two-hundred yards from here, if that's all the further you can kick my ass, you better be practicing your kicking." She ignored him, got the spare picks from the glove box in her car and headed back to the Blue Rose. She left Chet, hands on hips, standing in the middle of the parking lot doing his best to stare holes through her.

The second set was under way and Rhonda was glad she took the time to get her extra picks. She liked the style of hers better than the borrowed one and the chords seemed to come easier. Her pick danced over the steel strings and she realized she didn't have to worry about soft fingertips. She was relaxed and having fun.

She stopped in the middle of a down stroke, because Buster came huffing across the dance floor and leaped onto the stage. He grabbed the microphone and shouted into it. "Don't nobody leave this here place. We got us another murder out in the parkin' lot."

"Who the hell is it this time, Sheriff?" someone in the crowd shouted.

"Chet Longstreet's done been stabbed in the chest. Just like Sam Barstow was." He turned to Rhonda and said, "An' this time, little Missy, you ain't got no alibi. I seen him and you go out the front door together. You come back in, but Chet didn't. I went out there and there he was, bleeding like a stuck pig and dead as dead can be."

The sheriff dragged Rhonda off to jail. "Damn," he said to his deputy. "They ain't no direct evidence linking her to the killing. No blood on her clothes. Did you find anything at the parking lot?"

"Searched all over that parking lot and her car," the deputy said. "Didn't turn up the murder weapon, either."

The sheriff exhaled a loud grunt. "You can go…fer now," he said to Rhonda adding the same old warning about not leaving town.

* * *

Another week. Another Saturday night. Little if anything changed. Two men dead and Sheriff Buster didn't have a clue about who did the killings. Rhonda was on the stage again and the band was nearing the end of the last set of music. Ted slipped to the side of the platform and handed Rhonda a new bottle of water. She nodded a *thank you* to him and unscrewed the cap. It came off easier than usual, but she thought little of it. A couple of swigs and she was back into the music.

Tonight, Rhonda decided to take her guitar home with her, so when the music ended she slipped it into the soft case and started for her station wagon. Reaching the car she lifted the back door and slid the guitar inside. She turned around and was surprised to see Ted.

"How'd the water taste, Rhonda?" he said.

She took another swig, thought about the loosened cap and told him the water was okay. But she wondered. She looked at Ted, then at the water bottle and realized something was wrong. "How did you get out here so fast?" she said.

Ted grinned. "There's a trapdoor behind the bar. It goes down to our cold storage area and from there I can slip out the cellar's storm door on the side of the building. That's how I got out here the last two Saturday nights without being seen." His grin turned to a frown. "Rhonda, I want you. I've done so much for you. Will you marry me?"

Her head felt light and her knees were turning to rubber. "Marry you? We don't even date—how can I marry you?"

"If I can't have you, nobody will," he said.

She saw the knife in his hand and he was advancing toward her. What the hell can I do, she thought. I can't run on these legs. By now, Ted was about five feet from her. She leaned back and sat on the rear lip of the wagon's storage area. Her hand groped behind her and landed on the neck of the guitar. Rhonda pushed herself to a standing position dragging the Gibson behind her. She brought it up, took a two-hand grip on the neck and swung it with all her might. The guitar body caught Ted flush on the side of his head with the crunch of breaking wood and the twang of steel strings coming loose.

Rhonda slumped to the ground, her head resting against the car's back bumper. She heard people running across gravel, but couldn't concentrate. The blackness receded, the world came back into focus, and she saw Sheriff Buster Richfield waving a hand in front of her face. The ammonia from the capsule in the sheriff's hand jarred her wide-awake.

Buster said, "Well, little lady, I guess you solved the killin's. That knife ol' Ted was a carryin' shore does look like it could be the murder weapon. Guess forensics'll tell the tale."

Rhonda nodded and smiled a weak smile at him. It's time to shake the dust of this place off my jeans, she thought. Her mind was already planning the route she would take to get to the Big City.

THE END